To Lynn
with best wishes from
Mary (Cummins.)

HEIR TO BALGENNAN

Elizabeth Colville, accompanied by a woman
servant and a small party of horsemen, set out
from Wrykin Hall in Cumberland to travel to
Balgennan in South-West Scotland, where Elizabeth is pledged to marry her Cousin Archibald.
News is brought to Wrykin by Gavin Johnson,
Squire to Balgennan, that the party did not
arrive, and only one man was found dead of
head injuries.

Elizabeth's twin, Margaret, is determined to
take her sister's place as Archibald's bride, and
equally determined to find out what happened to
her sister. Scotland has lived through a troubled
part of its history, but King James I is determined to bring law and order to his country,
and to force the clans to live in harmony. His
punishment for disloyalty to the Crown is severe,
and Margaret finds that her husband, Sir
Archibald Johnson, has been involved in activities which could cost them their lives.

Margaret has to learn to live with this fear,
and the fear of some strange unknown creature
which attacks travellers if they venture too near
the sea.

MARY CUMMINS

HEIR TO BALGENNAN

ROBERT HALE · LONDON

© Mary Cummins 1978

First published in Great Britain 1978

ISBN 0 7091 6853 5

Robert Hale Limited
Clerkenwell House
Clerkenwell Green
London EC1R 0HT

Printed in Great Britain by Bristol Typesetting Co. Ltd,
Barton Manor, St. Philips, Bristol

ONE

Margaret Colville marvelled that so much beauty could hold so much cruelty. The sea was calm and peaceful, the hills a dim outline against the deep blue of the sky. The sun dipped lower, running long scarlet fingers along the coastline and turning the sea into a vast scarlet pool, and she again experienced the horror which had gripped her that other time, a sennight ago, when she could feel Elizabeth calling for her help and protection.

Margaret had almost sunk to a stupor, while the huge log fire blazed in the Great Hall, and her mother had ordered a posset to be brought, and Sarah Cowan to loosen her stays.

" It is not to be wondered that you miss your sister," she said, slapping Margaret's hands rather pettishly. " Twins with but a half-hour between the birthing, but this is poor bravery, Miss. Your sister is now wife to Sir Archibald Johnson of Balgennan Castle, a home worthy of her as I know myself, having been brought up within its walls. Your good father, Sir John, will soon find you a husband, never fear, even if the dowry is small, but with the Johnson fairness of face it should be easy."

Lady Mary Colville kept up her prattle even as she commanded Sarah to wet Mistress Margaret's lips, and sponge her forehead with her own blend of herbs sprinkled in water.

" There be more to it, my Lady," said Sarah, getting up off her knees from beside the long wooden settle where they had laid Margaret. " It's as . . . as though the Devil was possessing her . . ."

5

She crossed herself and Lady Mary struck her a blow on her ear.

"Hold your tongue, woman. There is no one more the angel . . ."

"Miss Elizabeth was the angel, but Miss Margaret . . . she is full of . . . of spirit," she ended, lamely.

The two young mistresses had looked as alike as two peas, but the elder one, Elizabeth, had been a quiet ladylike little female from the time she could walk. It was Miss Margaret who had kept her running about like a bantam hen.

Margaret was moaning a little, coming round.

"There is trouble . . . and danger . . . I can feel it. There is evil all round me."

"Hush your noise," said Lady Mary, half-fearfully. The younger of her twin daughters alarmed her sorely, but it was easy to see the reason for her discomfort. The twin children had never been parted, and now Margaret had grown desolate without her sister. So, too, was she missing Bessie Laird who had wet-nursed the babes when her own child died, and had stayed on in the household to help rear the infants and bring them to womanhood.

When Elizabeth had to leave her home in Cumberland to wed into Balgennan in Southern Scotland, Lady Mary had sent Bessie with her, fearing the harshness of sudden change for her daughter. It had not been easy to see her child go, even in the company of three strong men of their household, and with the promise of further escort beyond the Border.

Soon the men would return with a message to say that all was well, and Mistress Elizabeth happy in her new household. It was not too easy to place a female of small dowry and lesser power in a position higher than that into which she had been born, and they had been glad to accept the offer from Balgennan.

"Where is thy good sense?" she asked, sharply. "If you've lost it, Miss, then I can find the blow to sting your ears into bringing it back."

Margaret bit her lip. She saw the serving woman retreating

6

from her with something like fear in her eyes and she realised that the sensations of evil and nameless horror were only within herself.

" I beg pardon, Ma'am," she said to her mother. " It's but sorrow for the loss of company of my sister, I doubt not. I'll go to my room and rest a while if you will excuse me."

" Bed her for a day," Lady Mary ordered Sarah, " then we will have nothing more than good sense."

Several days later two strangers rode into the courtyard of Wrykin Hall followed by a small party of men, and Margaret could see at once that they were from Scotland by their mode of dress. One was young, and though but plain of clothing, he carried a good broadsword and rode with authority. Margaret learned that the young rider was an esquire called Gavin Johnson, in the service of the Earl of Balgennan, Sir Archibald's father, before she was ordered to retire from the room. Squire Johnson asked to see Sir John, then Lady Mary was admitted to the room where Sir John received his men of business, and a great cry was heard through the Great Hall.

Sir John called for Sarah Cowan and Margaret insisted on accompanying the serving woman. So it was that she learned of her sister's complete disappearance, along with three members of the party which accompanied her, Bessie Laird and two of the men. The escort from Balgennan had looked for them in vain at an Inn where they were expected to rest one night, and only one man had been found, his head cleaved open as he lay near the sands in a heap of bushes. They had stumbled on him in the darkness and Gavin Johnson had carried him back to Balgennan, but he had died before his tale could be told.

Gavin Johnson had told this part of his own tale with a show of reluctance.

" You know more than you tell us, Squire Johnson," said Margaret, striding forward.

Strangely, now that the worst was known, she had thrown off her dark mood of depression and a wild light shone in her eyes.

7

Gavin Johnson turned to look at his young kinswoman. His father was cousin to the Earl of Balgennan and he was as much related to this family as to the Earl.

"There are always mystery tales arising from the sea in my homeland, Mistress," he told her gravely. "It has been known for travellers to be lost before."

"Why, then, were you not more careful of my sister's welfare?" asked Margaret, and he coloured deeply so that she felt her arrow had gone home.

But he had drawn himself up proudly, his hand on the hilt of his sword which gave him the status he now held, and she saw that though he was plainly dressed, he held himself well and was not afraid of a straight look in the eye.

"I was required to escort Mistress Elizabeth from an Inn well-known to us as a place of shelter and safety. The escort with Mistress Elizabeth was well informed and instructed to stay at the Inn."

Sir John Colville was nodding since he, himself, had passed on these strict instructions to the men.

"But the lady was impatient of the hospitality."

"My sister was not used to rough dealings," said Margaret, and Gavin paused, looking at her thoughtfully under lowered brows.

"Mistress Elizabeth was warm and comfortably housed and well fed with rich foods, but she was impatient of waiting a few hours for . . . for my arrival. I kept to my time properly, but when I reached the Inn, the guid wife said her Ladyship had insisted on leaving near sundown and two of her men had drunk our ale, being unused to the stronger body of it."

"So your Innkeeper permitted my sister's men to fill themselves drunk," said Margaret, scornfully. "A fine protection for her!"

"Not so. It was but an aid to a night's sleep after fatigue if the young Mistress had but allowed it. She would take no heed of advice. It was not wise to go abroad by nightfall," said Gavin, quietly, "even with a party of strong arms instead of one, and two others in their cups. The one who rode bravely to her defence had been knocked into a hidden hollow, where

8

we might not have discovered him but for one of our horses rearing in fright. We tried valiantly to learn more from the man who escaped by some miracle, but he was too sore wounded to tell us anything."

" Then she could be alive," cried Lady Mary, " since no trace of her has been found. Our daughter could still be alive!"

Margaret again experienced the heaviness and horror which had surrounded her for the past few days, and the coldness of spirit which, to her, meant death.

" She is dead," she said flatly. " I know it."

" I fear Mistress Margaret is right. We . . . we have reason to believe this is so."

" What reason?" demanded Sir John, and it was a moment before Gavin answered.

" There was blood on the sands," he said, quietly. " We have seen the blood-marked sands before . . ."

" Your fine Border raiders," cried Margaret, but Gavin shook his head.

" The Borderers ride horseback at night, and take cattle and sheep, and leave a few blazing bonfires behind them. This . . . this is different. This is no known enemy."

Something in his tone made Margaret shiver and she saw her father glance fearfully at the young Squire. It was known that evil was abroad which was not the work of common men, and there seemed to be a pocket of evil lying perilously close to where her sister had been sent to bide after marriage.

Suddenly Margaret was weary, having chased sleep for too many nights.

" I would ask permission to retire," she begged her father, then bobbed to her mother and to the squire as permission was given.

Margaret swept gracefully from the chamber, and held herself strong and upright till she reached the sanctuary of her own bedroom, where she collapsed in a storm of tears.

" I will find thy murderers, Elizabeth," she cried aloud. " They shall not go unpunished. I will let thee live, in me, until

A*   9 they are crying for mercy. Never fear, my dove. They will suffer three times for your own suffering."

Listening at the door, Sarah Cowan hurried away and began to hustle up the wayward household maids and men-servants to provide food and shelter for the Balgennan Squire and his escort. Yet there was fear in her heart as she felt the touch of the unknown, almost like a feather against her cheek. What did the strange girl, Mistress Margaret, see that was not already to be seen by everybody else? If she had been born of common people, she would have been classed as a witch.

*   *   *

Margaret kept to her room as much as possible, pacing up and down with long mannish strides, hands hugging her arms as though to afford protection from her thoughts.

Gavin Johnson had been asked to stay a few days to rest himself and his men, but after only one day which he employed in checking horses and equipment, he asked leave of his host to ride for the Borders the following morning.

" There are matters of importance my master would discuss with members of the Privy Council, and one or two of them he would entertain at Balgennan before they are called to Parliament, so I must beg leave, if you please. My regret is that my errand was such a one as to cast sorrow over the visit. It's seldom I cross the Border now that I am squired to Balgennan."

Margaret had watched his tall, stalwart figure striding round the courtyard. Soon he would be gone, and with him the only contact she had with the fate of her sister. Yet Margaret was seething inside with questions as she fought the devils which tormented her, urging her to do something about it, and not let it all rest and slip away to forgetfulness.

Slowly the thoughts and plans which had come to her were building up inside, unwilling to be dismissed lightly, yet needing strength to force her will on others. She would have the approval of no one, of that she was well assured.

Lady Mary sent a message that her presence would be required at table, since their guest was not likely to sup with them beyond this one evening, and Margaret rose and selected a long plain white dress, with a silver cross on a chain round her neck. Then she descended the wide stone stairs to the large cold draughty hall, its flagged floor clean and freshly strewn, and a large log fire burning brightly and giving a semblance of heat and comfort.

The squire did not rate higher than pewter, but this was well embossed and of quality workmanship. Mistress Margaret took her place at the table, and looked again at the young squire, whose face was red with heat, he having had his chair placed nearest the fire as a mark of deference to him as a guest.

" So you go tomorrow, Kinsman," said Margaret, and her father frowned. Elizabeth had been quiet and dignified at the entertainment of guests, but Margaret did not have the reticence usually attributed to young unmarried females.

" Aye, Mistress," he replied. " We ride after dawn."

" I beg leave to ride with you, Sir," said Margaret, quietly.

There was stunned silence, then Sir John's brows drew together with menace.

" Lady Mary, our daughter has lost her manners," he said coldly. " I think she may be excused."

" Please, I beg, let me finish," said Margaret. " The Earl asked for one of us, Elizabeth or myself, to wed with his son. There was no wedding, so no law could prevent me from wedding with my sister's betrothed if no ceremony took place. I . . . I would ask to take my sister's place. Sir Thomas did not specify which one of us would make a fitting bride for his son. Elizabeth elected to go since she is . . . was . . . the elder. There is no reason why Sir Archibald cannot still have his bride."

" I will not countenance it," said Sir John.

He had no wish to insult a guest, but having lived under English rule for a great many years, he was feeling more and more that the Scots were barbarous and not to be trusted. At present there was peace on the Borders, with the exception of a few skirmishings, but he had pondered deeply before he allowed Elizabeth to go. He loved his son, James, and daughters were well in their way, but in his heart he admired the pride and courage of this other daughter, Margaret, and deeply lamented that she had not been another boy.

There was much to recommend Margaret's scheme, not the least being her willingness for the marriage, and he knew that Sir Thomas Johnson would find pleasure in it. It would be an open statement that there was still trust between the families.

" If you think well of it in a sennight, Father," said Margaret, coaxingly, " it may well be with regrets."

Sir John stroked his chin and saw that the Squire was looking stubborn with disapproval.

" It lends itself ill to our guest," he said, heavily, and again Gavin coloured.

" I would consult with my master before such decisions are made," he said, rather sullenly.

" It is true that Sir Thomas may ill like this change without his authority," Sir John conceded, musingly.

" Then I am willing that I should return unwed," put in Margaret, though her eyes glinted as though saying that such a thing was more than unlikely.

" The journey is unsafe, as judge by thy sister," said Gavin.

" I will be safe with you," said Margaret, sweetly.

" You will need a serving woman."

" I will take Sarah Cowan."

Sarah Cowan, hovering within hearing distance, felt her heart turn to ice. She would flee from Wrykin Hall first! She would creep out silently after all was abed. Her eyes grew enormous at the thought, as she squeezed herself behind a wall hanging and tried to push away the waves of terror. She would risk the same fate as Bessie Laird if she went with Mistress Margaret. Yet she was not free, and had nowhere to go. She would entreat Lady Mary for clemency.

" We leave before sunrise," said Gavin Johnson, crisply. " We must arrive at each Inn to rest well before nightfall."

" Never fear, I can ride with any man. You will not be

delayed because of *me*. And I acknowledge your authority on the journey."

"So be it," said Gavin, and asked leave to retire. He almost collided with Sarah Cowan who was hovering in the shadows, and he could smell the sour odour of her fear. His own was half-way as bad.

TWO

That night the household at Wrykin Hall was late abed, the servants being sent scurrying to prepare the packing for the journey, supervised by Lady Mary and the Squire. It was essential that they travelled lightly, yet a certain amount of comfort was needed since Margaret was unused to journeys which took longer than a few hours.

Lady Mary had been selective in the choice of friends for her daughters and had been ever zealous that they did not learn rough manners. Looking at Margaret she wondered afresh at her younger twin daughter, as the young woman ordered some of the servants to make more haste, and bullied Sarah Cowan into better behaviour.

" I thought better of you, Sarah," she said. " A jellyfish would show more spirit. Are you grown woman or infant? There is neither husband nor child to keep you here at Wrykin."

Gavin Johnson had watched her imperious authority, his eyes hooded and inscrutable, and sometimes Lady Mary's heart misgave her. A nightmare had descended on their family, but Border families learned to live with nightmares when the sky would be lit with the blaze of bonfires and there would be a smell of burning and cries of wounded men and women after a raid, when homes would be plundered and women raped, and children carried off to slave for their food and drink.

At last the household was quiet, while a few hours rest were snatched by the travellers. Sir John Colville lay sleepless, his mind turning over the decision he had taken. His had been the final word, but he felt, rather uneasily, that it had been made for him. Lady Mary, tired out by making these new arrangements, slept at last. Soon her grief would be spent, and Sir John would bring their son home and find a wife for him. There would be new life at Wrykin, and Margaret's decision to go to Balgennan was her own. One must live one's life, and trust in God.

For the first hour's ride, Margaret held herself aloof from Gavin Johnson, making Sarah Cowan ride with her, though after a time the older woman fell behind, while Gavin rode at the head of their small party, then he in turn fell back, and rode beside Margaret.

Though still sorely troubled by her sister's death, the early morning sea air was invigorating and brought a sparkle to her eyes and cheeks. The sea was calm but ablaze with diamond lights in the sunshine, as they followed the shore, then turned in-country towards the Border city of Carlisle.

Margaret had only heard about Scotland from tales told by her parents, and they were not always gentle stories. She imagined it as a barren country, wild and barbarous, with marshy lands, so that it gave her no small surprise to see very little change in the scenery as they rested at the first Scottish Inn chosen by the Squire. Margaret could even see primroses and shy violets growing under nearby trees, as she was helped from her mount, whilst listening to the low mumblings of Sarah Cowan.

"Hold thy tongue, woman," she said, wearily. "Let thy stomach talk for you after our host has brought good plain fare. Obey Squire Gavin and forget thy fears. The escort is well chosen."

Gavin, over-hearing, said nothing but felt no small pleasure in the remark. He had been circumspect over his treatment of Mistress Margaret, unsure of her temper and of her future position with regard to Balgennan. A wasp-tongued woman could do more to give a man small comfort than a sword thrust against the hindquarters.

"So you are unafraid now that you are in barbarous

country, Mistress Margaret," he remarked when they had eased themselves and were awaiting food and drink. "You must know that our ways are foreign to the gentlemen and our manners uncouth to the ladies. Worse still, we put pretty maidens in the soup pot and stand gentle lads to guard over them that they might cook them to a turn."

Margaret could see the twinkle in his eyes. The Scots were ever ready to turn their own rough ways into wit of a kind.

"I shall test the last plump miss to be so used with true interest, so be my stomach as empty," she replied, equably, and he laughed heartily so that she liked the merriment on his face.

"I was afeared of dry brown hills and dank marshes," she said, looking out of the small space which served as a window at the Inn. It was built in recent times and mainly of wood, since many Inns on the Borders were razed by fire more than once in their existence. The landlord and wife, knowing no other way of life, removed their items of worth, then rebuilt their Inn getting labour as they could, and proudly stating all the new improvements from the old place which was like to fall down had the torches missed their target.

"We have brown hills of dried bracken, and purple hills of rich heather, and woodland areas, rich crops, rich pastures, wild roses such as I see in your cheeks, wild violets such as Mistress Cowan might approve, and all manner of things you boast in England. We also have beggars and cut-throats and the lazy who would do nothing to earn their meat except steal from those who toil."

"Yet the King, himself, is barbarous and cruel to his nobles, as witness my Lord Murdoch, the Duke of Albany, the King's own kin."

"Ah now, Madam, if you try to talk treason, just remember that our good King James was a prisoner in England and grew up at the English Court. He is a cultured and educated man, a poet, a painter, a musician . . . and he married an English lady."

"Aye, the Lady Joan Beaufort."

Gavin's voice dropped and he looked at Margaret warningly. " Do not judge until your knowledge is at first hand, Mistress. The King has his reasons for what he did. He rules by Parliament and heeds not the prodding of his nobles who prod the less when they see he means what he says. A few heads rolling can keep others more wise on their owners' shoulders. The Duke of Albany ruled Scotland as The Guardian in our fathers' days, and ruled for his brother Robert III, who was old and gentle and sick, being kicked by a horse when a boy. But when Robert's eldest son, David, grew old enough to be Guardian on behalf of his father, Albany liked not to give up his role and it is a powerful thought that the Prince died in his youth at Falkland while Albany stood guard over him. There are whispers that he was starved to death . . . "

" Starved! My heavens! " said Margaret.

" Though the real truth is still a secret in the hearts of men gone to the grave. There are those who say that Rothesay . . . as was Prince David's title . . . was a wild one and not fit to be Guardian, and that Albany was only thinking of the Crown and his moral right to remove Rothesay if he would have made us a poor King. Then others say that he died of his own excesses. But our good King James the First, who was Rothesay's younger brother, was but a boy at the time and sent to France by his father for his own safety. But the sea gives frail security to a young Prince, even with strong attendants, and the English pirates captured him. It broke our old King's heart to have James imprisoned so. The boy was always his favourite."

Margaret listened, fascinated. She had heard snatches of gossip, but never the full tale of King James' capture and imprisonment in England. The gossip among the ladies had always been of the Lady Joan Beaufort who was in love with the young King of Scots, being held by King Henry IV to ransom, then by Henry V.

" There are those who say his ransom is even now only half paid," said Margaret.

" If you would be Mistress of Balgennan one day, the King will demand loyalty," said Gavin Johnson sternly. " Which country has your love and your heart? The country which held our King to ransom, or the country which he is now building as a land fair and free to live in?"

"But, is it free?" asked Margaret, sweetly, "when my sister and her party can vanish for ever? When bands of robbers must be guarded against?"

"Is any country free and safe?" countered Gavin. "Is Scotland? England? France? Are the people happier in France than in Scotland?"

"There is new life rising in England, or so says my father and brother who has been sent away to school at Windsor, and will go on to College at Oxford. He is a scholar as well as a brave boy, and no longer should a strong sword-arm determine how well we run our lands."

"Then show thy pride in our own College at St. Andrews, where your own children may be educated. They will no longer be sent to France for education. It is well for us to have talked, Mistress Margaret, before we reach Balgennan and you meet my Lord, the Earl, once again. He will accept thy pride and loyalty in Balgennan which is a sweet Earldom."

"And yours, if my husband-to-be, Sir Archibald, succumbs to his wounds. Is it not so, Squire Gavin? I know of your kinship."

"Then know, also, that my father already owns Nithrie which will be mine one day. True, it is poor land and small, besides Balgennan, but we love every blade of grass, every sour sod in every field, and when I win my spurs I will gain more land to sweeten my acres. I have no need of Balgennan, Mistress, and grudge it not to Sir Archibald. If you had not forced my hand in bringing you with me, I may have spent a day at Nithrie . . ."

Squire Johnson's colour was high in his cheeks and his words tumbled out angrily while he glared at Margaret. Then, as suddenly, the anger went out of him and he rose and stamped about the room.

"Landlord" he yelled. "Must thee kill the animal and skin it before bringing it to the table? Dost take all day?"

The servants were scurrying at the sound of authority and

Margaret could hear Sarah Cowan's shrill laughter in a back room, and the deep tones of their henchmen. No doubt news and gossip had been holding up the Innkeeper and his wife, as it had Gavin Johnson and herself. She should feel tired, but instead the blood ran warmly in her veins and she felt the pangs of hunger.

"What manner of man is Sir Archibald?" she asked, and Gavin turned cold eyes on her.

"I am a servant of Sir Thomas, and doing the job he set me, and one which you have forced upon me. I trust that escorting you, a twin sister of Sir Archibald's bride-to-be, will not be thought to be beyond my duties. If so, he will be no bridegroom of thine. So I tell you to wait till we reach Balgennan, then find out for thyself."

Margaret said nothing. For the first time her heart was growing cold at her own temerity. Was she mad that she should push herself forward as a bride, and insist on taking her sister's place? From her short conversation with Sir Gavin, she was realising that there were things to be learned about this new country, things of which she had been completely ignorant, even though her family still considered themselves mainly Scots.

"We will talk again, Squire Gavin," she said, rather imperiously.

"If your tongue be as busy after filling your stomach, then you must silence it in sleep," he told her. "Tomorrow we ride through Galloway."

"Shall I see the Solway again?"

"That you will, then along the coastline to Balgennan, south of Ayr. The Royal Burgh of Ayr is fine enough, even for thee, and is but an hour's ride from Balgennan."

"And the sea?"

"Lashes on the rocks beneath the old Castle. Rest easy. The sound of the ocean will be thy lullaby . . ."

He stopped, the ready colour again in his cheeks.

"And Sir Archibald?"

"He is sick of his wounds. I told thee. He will not be thy bedfellow for some weeks, wed or not."

"But he is a brave knight, and courteous to a lady?"

"Use your tongue on the meat," he told her, curtly. "Our ladies do not clack-clack all day lest it be among themselves. It wearies my head."

She bit back an acid reply. Squire Gavin would listen to her after she had authority over him, and time would take care of that.

*   *   *

On the following morning, Margaret was in a sober mood again as they rode into the wild Galloway countryside. The freshness of spring sunshine had changed to lowering clouds and bursts of rain windblown against the hood of her cloak. She bent her head against the discomfort of the day and had no cheer in her when Gavin Johnson rode ahead, then back, to say that the roadway was clear of water and they may keep to the trodden way. Sometimes the road ran parallel to the sea, and Margaret rode more slowly, staring at the lashing waves breaking against the rocks. Suddenly she was feeling the same inner chill which had assailed her when she felt that Elizabeth was in some kind of danger.

"Show me the spot where it was last known that my sister was alive. Show me where the henchman was found injured."

"It will serve nothing, Mistress," said Gavin, tersely. "It profits nothing to dwell on such things. Keep your sister alive in your heart. It is better so."

"I would care to see the place," she insisted and he shrugged.

"So be it."

After about twenty minutes' riding they passed a douce Inn, well-kept and tidy.

"We will eat here, if thee can stomach it. It is the last Inn which housed Mistress Elizabeth."

Margaret rode slowly up to the courtyard.

"I can stomach it," she said, quietly, and Gavin Johnson's eyes gleamed strangely.

"Oh, Mistress Margaret, let us ride on," pleaded Sarah Cowan. "I like it not here, sweet though it be."

"Your stomach will be all the sweeter for some good meat," said Margaret, rather grimly. "It is my pleasure to see the landlord and his good wife."

"We will ask no questions, Squire Gavin, until I see what manner of wife the good woman makes to her landlord."

"So be it, Mistress Margaret."

He went to give orders to their escort and to see that the horses were receiving attention, then escorted Margaret into the Inn, while Sarah Cowan followed behind them, hobbling a little and looking around at the dwelling apprehensively. Unlike some they had passed, it was built of stone and not turf, and seemed more prosperous than those which only afforded shelter for the night and enough sustenance to keep strength in the body, without pandering to taste. In this Inn there was a smell of good meat baking, and tasty fruit pies.

The landlord had taken a quick look at Margaret, his face blanching, and she stared at him, her head thrown back and her eyes bold. This was where Elizabeth was last known to be alive and well, though already he had been questioned well by the local magistrate to whom Balgennan had made a strong complaint, and who had descended with his men to pull the countryside apart.

Now Margaret saw a flash of fear on the landlord's face, and a gasp from his wife as she moved forward to stare at the girl, her face rosy from the fire, a white cap fallen sideways a little over her abundant black hair.

Then she and her husband were looking at one another, and it seemed to Margaret that their faces were lit by a new inner joy.

"Och, but the young Mistress is hame after a'," the woman said, beaming, as she came forward. "The Lord be thanked. We were afeared my guid man would be dangling like others before us."

"What do you mean by that?" asked Margaret, motioning Sarah forward to remove her cloak.

21

The woman was too happy to be reticent.

"The Innkeepers here aboots. Travellers get lost . . . lose their way or . . . or worse!" For a moment her voice dropped. "Then the landlord gets the blame. I kenned they would be here blaming Will some time, and they did, Mistress, when it was yourself that went astray. We were feared he would be hard pressed keeping heid to body, if the sheriff's men came back. Och, but I've never been sae glad to see a lady before. Ye'll have the best this hoose can provide . . ."

"You mistake me, good wife," said Margaret, sitting down on a wooden chair by the fireside. "I am paying my first visit to the Inn. The lady you saw before was my sister. I was born within the hour after her. My sister is . . . is still missing . . ."

The light went out of the woman's face, and she looked at her husband.

"We ken nowt about her, Mistress," he said, and Margaret saw honesty in his eyes. "There's troubled times here, and queer strange things that are not the work o' the Good Lord, though we keep His Spirit alive in this hoose. The Devil rides awa' wi' senseless folk that go abroad in the twilight. The darkness can swallow them so that there's nowt more heard o' them, and honest folks are getting blamed. Where could I hide a party o' folks so that nowt is seen o' them ever again? Could I dig graves even while I serve ale? Could my guid wife wear their fine garments and make them look like her own? There's a law in the land against the wearing o' fine silks for folk like us. Could she hide the spoils o' booty just for her own pleasure and risk being hanged and her body left to rot as a warning? Others have suffered that punishment whom we kenned were innocent. If we are blamed but one more time, then we maun creep away in the night and leave our Inn, that has taken our lives and our hearts to build up."

He was appealing both to Gavin and Margaret, even as his wife was bringing forward a white scrubbed table and setting it with hot broth and a piece of bread, which was a dainty, so that their comfort by the fireside was not disturbed.

" And you have no idea as to what fate was in store for my sister?" asked Margaret.

She saw the glance of fear pass between husband and wife again. They knew something, or suspected it. Of that she was sure.

She was also becoming more convinced that Gavin Johnson had not been responsible in any way for Elizabeth's disappearance. It had happened to many people before her. Unless . . . unless Gavin knew that, and had taken advantage of it.

She glanced at his face, and saw now that it was open and honest, well-coloured and handsome. Could he be driven by ambition to commit murder? On the journey they had talked together, and she was beginning to feel liking and trust in her heart for him. Had he been her bridegroom she would have been content, she confessed to herself, always willing to face an issue with honesty. Gavin would make a fine husband.

But her cousin, Archibald, would be her partner and he was the Balgennan heir, and no doubt brave since he was recovering from his wounds after his last battle. He had obeyed a call by the Crown to fight in France for England, as part of the treaty, still being paid, for the return of their King.

" Have you no children?" she asked the wife.

" A lass married to a farmer, and a lad, good with his bow and arrow," she said, proudly. " Last holiday when the men shot their three arrows at the target beside the Parish Kirk, he was better than his father."

" Gie me a good pike or axe," said the landlord, " and I'll knock heids wi' the best of them."

" And gie us our horses," said Gavin, rising. " Refresh thyself, Mistress, if the guid wife will but show you where, and we'll ride for Balgennan. There's plenty of time till sundown, but we'll be on our way."

Margaret rose and followed the landlady, Sarah close at her heels, and they refreshed themselves and washed their hands and faces, drying with rough cloth, but clean. The Inn was comfortable, but apart from the bread, there was no daintiness and Margaret had to use her own rose-scented water to ease the smell of travel.

" The Devils that are abroad . . . they cam' frae the sea. Mind the sea, Mistress," the guid wife whispered as they were about to leave.

" Do you mean in ships?"

" No, no. It's no' anything you can see. There's no sign o' ships or boats or suchlike. Just . . . just blood on the sand whiles."

Margaret swallowed.

" Like a sea monster?" she asked.

" Once or twice a footprint, but no beasties. A bare foot, like . . . like a bairn's."

" A bairn's! You mean . . . a child?"

" Aye, Mistress. A wee bairn."

" Couldn't it be from a missing child?" asked Margaret.

" No, no. Travelling bairns are a' happed up, and few o' them. This was a *bare* foot. A wee bare foot. A bairn's."

Margaret could feel the shiver of the unknown turning her stomach to ice.

" Did thee tell Squire Johnson?" she asked.

" No, only thyself, Mistress. Some o' the men . . . they think our heids have gone sick. But I tell thee, Mistress, I have seen them myself. Wee bairns' feet and the red stains o' blood on the sands afore the tide got in to wash it away as though it had never been. And . . . and worse, Mistress . . ."

Her voice dropped even lower.

" We've seen limbs washed up wi' the bits o' wood we pick up by the shore."

" Limbs! "

" Aye, legs an' arms. Torn off bodies, and picked dry o' the flesh. As though the craws had got at them, though we maun kill the craws that nest in the trees or pay a fine o' five shilling if we maun fell the tree instead. The wapinschaw was only last month when we showed our weapons and showed that we had killed our young craws, so it was not the craws, Mistress."

Margaret's head was beginning to reel. She must ask Gavin about a wapinschaw, and learn about the laws which seemed strange to her. At the moment she could not seem to take in the significance of all the landlady was telling her, and her tales of small footprints, seen before the tide rushed away the evidence, and limbs picked dry of flesh, was more like a good horror tale for a winter's evening when a warm family sat round a blazing log fire, or the coal such as they used in Scotland.

"For thy ear alone, Mistress," the wife was saying. "It's no' to be bandied aboot."

Margaret nodded and wrapped herself in her cloak. She was now convinced that the woman was either a born story-teller or the tales of disappearing travellers was affecting her strangely.

"What is a wapinschaw?" she asked Gavin, as they rode forward again.

"It is a meeting where all men are called from town and country to show that they hold the correct weapons according to their station in life. Every man must learn to fight, every man from sixteen to sixty, and must have weapons according to rank. We hold four wapinschaws each year."

"And you must kill young crows?"

Gavin looked at her and grinned.

"Women's gossip has its surprises," he said. "I would have expected the latest English cloth would have been a curiosity to our good landlady since it is different from her own weave. There's been little buying and selling over the Borders since the last packman was caught and hanged."

Margaret was not smiling. They had come to a rocky shore-line and again she felt the coldness, almost of Death, within her so that her limbs felt heavy and her breathing shallow. All around her was great natural beauty of pale spring sun-shine against sparkling waves, and the fresh green of country-side, with hazy purple of distant mountains. Gavin breathed the pure air into his lungs with appreciation.

"It is near here that you found your henchman," said Margaret, and he stared at her.

"Aye, Not far. How come you know that, Mistress?"

She shivered. Was she being influenced by the land-lady's weird tales? There was no trace of blood on the sands now, and no white limbs lying among the flotsam washed up by the sea. Yet the place held an oppression for her.

"Let us ride on, Master Gavin," she said. "I would reach Balgennan as soon as may. My uncle may not like the plans to be put to him."

"I don't like them myself, Mistress Margaret."

"Then you'll say why not."

He shook his head, and looked straight at her.

"A squire has no room for personal feelings. My mislike is for what I feel in my own heart, and is not my right to dis-cuss with thee."

Margaret bit her lip. Suppose Sir Thomas refused to acknowledge her, and his son spurned her. It might be weeks before Squire Gavin could arrange to escort her home again to Wrykin Hall.

She dropped back a little to ride beside Sarah Cowan.

"I deserve thy hand on my buttocks, Sarah," she said morosely, "as was usual when I was but child, and you our good nurse."

Immediately Sarah's protective love was to the fore.

"I'll stay by thee, Mistress," she said, "never fear."

"Good Sarah. I'm going to need thy help and succour."

They had come within sight of the large crenellated castle on the coast which was Balgennan, and Margaret's heart was caught by its grandeur and the richness of the surrounding countryside. Men were working in the fields and cattle and sheep grazed peacefully. On the rocks beneath the castle walls, the sea was lashing, in a gentle mood, and Sarah looked at it with more pleasure.

"It is a sweet dwelling, Mistress," she said.

Gavin had ridden on to prepare the way, and as they rode over the drawbridge into the courtyard, men ran forward to help the party to dismount, and an elderly man with greying hair came out from one of the small chambers built into the curtain of the castle. He had the look of her mother, but he seemed years older than she remembered.

He said nothing till he had come close to Margaret, then his eyes roamed over her from head to toe, seeing that she had grown to womanhood.

" I beg leave to take my sister's place," she said, clearly, her chin stiff with nerves. " My father sends a letter. My sister and I are . . . were . . . of the same image, being twins born."

" You are brave, Mistress," said Sir Thomas Johnson. " You would venture out after thy sister has come to harm. But I accept you in her stead. The bargain is made, and I bid you welcome."

He came forward and kissed her on the forehead and both cheeks.

" You have done well, Gavin," he told the Squire. " I am pleased with thee."

The Squire's face had grown reserved, and he now looked at Margaret with impersonal but respectful eyes, as he bowed to her and Sir Thomas.

" I will give leave for extra guests at our table," said Sir Thomas, leading the way up broad stone stairs and into the Great Hall. " I will expect thee, Gavin."

" As it pleases," said Gavin, bowing.

Looking after him, Margaret felt she had lost a friend, and that the warm companionship which had been growing between them was no longer there.

Suddenly the old grey walls and stone floor was cold. Balgennan was large and impressive, but was not rich in soft grandeur.

But now she would be introduced to her bridegroom, the man with whom she must share the rest of her life, and her palms sweated nervously.

" Sir Archibald . . . is he here?" she asked, looking round.

Sir Thomas smiled, though this time his eyes were without humour.

" An eager bride indeed," he said. " My son is suffering of his wounds, but I will take thee to his chamber. I hope you'll find him a braw lad."

" Perhaps it's better that I change my garments. They are stained with the dust of travel," she said.

" My son will take no heed of a few particles of dust."

Sir Thomas had taken her up the spiral staircase to the living quarters, turning along another narrow passage. She learned that her rooms would be near at hand, and before she had time to reflect, a door had been thrown open, and she was shown into a chamber, heavy with the odour of sickness, malodorous wounds and jugs of wine and ale, with plates of half-eaten food.

" Find a servant to clean the pigsty," roared Sir Thomas. " My son keeps what he wants not till it rots."

" They hang like craven crows waiting for the spoils," grinned the figure on the bed. " So there's news for me of a bride after all. They say the Devil ran away with my last one, rather than let me have her."

Margaret was staring at the man on the bed, though he was little more than a boy. He was thin and unkempt. and almost emaciated as he reached out a claw-like arm to her. But his broad forehead and grinning mouth were almost bestial, so that she felt a sense of revulsion. She thought of Gavin Johnson who looked every inch a gentleman, and remembered how he misliked what she was doing. Why had he not told her, or prepared her for this repulsive boy who was leering at her and reaching out to stroke her white arm?

" I am pleased to make your acquaintance, Sir," she said, clearly. " Now I beg leave to be excused. My travel cloak is likely to soil everything it touches."

Sir Archibald threw back his head and laughed.

" Prim and proper, Mistress. We will excuse thee, I'm sure."

*   *   *

Margaret dined alone with Sir Thomas that evening, the meat being as dainty as she would have wished. Archibald was fed by a manservant in his room, but if the noises which came from his quarters were any indication, then his meat was more liquid than good hearty food. Margaret could hear his drunken voice railing at the servant and the sounds of things being thrown after the luckless man. Sir Thomas glowered, but made no comment.

Sarah Cowan came to help Margaret in her room, a small chamber but well appointed. The castle was L-shaped, with small chambers and her quarters would be changed after the wedding ceremony, or so Sir Thomas had informed her, and she would have accommodation more fitted to the Mistress of Balgennan, which title she would hold in the absence of a Countess.

She liked the small chamber with its view of the sea which lashed against the rocks so far below. The Castle had been built out on a rock so that it was protected on three sides by the sea. The day was clear and she could see the coastline of the Isle of Arran, its mountain peaks bluish-purple, while the rock known as Ailsa Craig towered out of the sea south of the Castle.

"Don't stay here, Mistress," Sarah Cowan pleaded as she ran to attend Margaret. "Thy bridegroom is ugly . . . and has a temper. If you want to see who has put away Mistress Elizabeth and our good Bessie Laird, my own friend, then we need look no further."

"Hush your wanderings," said Margaret, sharply.

"Why should he desire a bride then dispose of her without even sight of her? How could a sick man, confined to bed, vanquish my sister and our henchmen, some of the party being his own men? Better he does not have a bride at all, then murder would not be deemed necessary."

Sarah was momentarily put off, but already kitchen gossip had filled her mind.

"He wenches at the Fayre when he is better of his wounds. The good master, the Earl, is forcing him to take a wife and secure an heir?"

"Then why murder my sister? He had not even seen her."

"I know not. I grant you that. But a man like Sir Archibald needs no reason. The Devil speaks to him, Mistress Margaret.

Let us be gone with Master Gavin who is good and kind."

" He dare not have my death at his door," said Margaret,
with spirit. " If he be responsible for my sister's death, then I
shall find out. But he dared not be responsible for mine. The
King is a strong man, bringing law and order to this land, and
willing to hear complaint from all manner of peoples. I could
soon swear a complaint, and will not hesitate to do so, if I find
him guilty of . . . of Elizabeth's death."

Suddenly her courage was beginning to falter, and she
needed all her strength to go forward with resolution and finish
the task she had set out to do.

" Mistress Margaret," Sarah Cowan was saying, looking at
the girl's drooping figure. " I loved Mistress Elizabeth, and
perhaps served her before thee, but thy courage and valour
makes me serve you, come what may. Stay if you will, but
know that Sarah Cowan will lay down her life for you, on
that I lay my word and my reason."

" Oh, Sarah! "

The older woman's plump arms were round the young girl,
cradling her even as she wept for her sister and her situation.

" That Ailsa Craig . . . that rock . . . it is a prison," said
Sarah in a low voice. " They say that poor creatures are
rowed across and left on the rock. There is no means of return
except by boat, and if it displeased my Lord, or more likely
Sir Archibald, then the creatures are left there, sometimes to
starve. Take care, Mistress, that ye do not displease him."

Margaret started out over the sea at the bare rock. Was
that where Elizabeth had gone? she wondered.

Yet she'd had enough of Sarah's gloom, even though she
was glad of her presence in the house. She was too inclined
to listen to servants' gossip and believe all she was told.

" I shall wear my blue silk with the pearl trimming," said
Margaret, turning abruptly. " The fatigue of the journey has
turned thy brain. The Earl of Balgennan is as fine a gentleman
as any you would find at the Court of good King Henry, and
his son is but rough and ill-used because of the pain of his
wounds. Better he rant and swear at a servant than that he
scream with the agony of it. Honour him for bravery, as I

must honour him when the knot is tied. But . . . " her voice dropped, " if I find he has killed my sister, then 'fore God he shall pay, be he husband or no."

Sarah Cowan hurried to obey her, but this time she saw no witchery in her Mistress, only shining courage.

THREE

Squire Gavin had been sent out on lawful business so that he did not dine with Sir Thomas and Margaret, much to her secret disappointment.

"I trust my sister is happy now that Cumberland is under the English Crown, yet well-thinking people make it a good land and pleasant living. I had a meeting with your father, Sir John, some time ago when you were a child, as I remember, and we travelled together to York where we witnessed the York fishermen making merry and acting out a play, by name, 'The Flood' for our pleasure. Noah was a gentle fellow and his wife of shrewish temper, but their antics made laughter for us, and good humour. If a minstrel asks leave to play for us, or a beggar to earn his meat by telling a tale, we will enjoy their services for your benefit. I would not wish thee dull at Balgennan."

"It . . . it all looks very pretty," said Margaret, rather lamely.

"Aye, we follow fashion here as elsewhere. Our King learned much at the English Court, and glad we are to have him home these years, even though the Court gave us a fine bill for the expenses of keeping him and without invitation to do so. The years go by and we are still paying the sum. But King James is a brave man and fit to rule, not like his Cousin Murdoch, and not one merk would I pay for him, nor would have paid for him since his head was as like to wood as this table."

"We heard sad tales of Murdoch, Duke of Albany, and his family."

" I will tell thee the truth, then guard thy tongue, Mistress," said Sir Thomas, sternly. " There are those, and especially the Grahams, who would doubt the wisdom of our King and his handling of that family, but doubt not that King James handled the matter wisely. He is a fine man, educated to civil company, and not barbarous like some of our nobles. He can pluck music from the strings of his lute fit to make your heart weep, and he can paint a picture so that it might come to life if a man looks on it long enough. *And* write a poem to his Lady, his milk-white dove, Queen Johanna."

Margaret had sometimes heard gossip when she was invited to stay at Brougham, that the Lady Joan Beaufort, daughter of the Earl of Somerset, was no dove, but she said nothing.

" Why was he so set against Duke Murdoch?" asked Margaret, curious to hear Sir Thomas' view of the matter.

" James had no call to love Murdoch," said Sir Thomas. ' His father, King Robert III was too gentle to rule by strength, so Robert's brother, the Duke of Albany, was Guardian.

" Some of my own kind were willing to serve the King, James, but Murdoch and his ilk were like to go their own way and laugh at our King, so he made an example of them after much provocation, and he threw them into prison. But members of the family rose up against him, and he had to put them to death or rule like a weakened King. It must be the same laws for the nobles as for the common people who are being encouraged to keep our laws and make a sweet country to live in, with well-taught sons and daughters, and working farmers digging their plot of land every day, be he holder of oxen or not. The land grows good for cultivation and we feed our people."

" Yet my sister goes missing on her journey to Balgennan, even with armed escort."

" I know nought of what happened to the Mistress Elizabeth, and I did not fail in my duty to seek for her, and to report her loss to the magistrates. She disobeyed our orders and should not have ridden after nightfall."

" Cannot the good new laws help to protect people after nightfall?"

" It is easy to say ' Aye ' to new laws when they are debated in Parliament, but not so easy to enforce them," said Sir Thomas, rather tiredly. " We have beggars abroad and they would murder for their own gain. We passed a law that a beggar must be licensed and wear a badge, but beggars are lawless people and who can make them law-abiding? I tell you, beggars killed your sister."

" And took her away without trace?"

" Aye, there you have it," Sir Thomas agreed. " It has happened before. Sooner or later we will find the foul fiends responsible. In the meantime, you are a brave woman to take your sister's place.

" The priest will call on Friday. The marriage can take place by my son's sick-bed. It is usual in these times when young nobles are wounded in battle. The battle wounds often lend the greater pride and pleasure to a good match. They are not to be looked on with shame."

" Is . . . is Sir Archibald like to be better soon of his wounds?" asked Margaret.

The Earl gazed at her sombrely.

" A good wife can often harry a doctor into making more effort to speed the poison. I do not like the wounds as they are now, Mistress Margaret. Do your best when the knot is tied. Take command of the sick room. Help my son to . . . to eat better and not to depend on his wines to dull the pain. Order the servants to clean and poultice the wounds."

" I will do what I can," Margaret told him, and he nodded.

" Was Mistress Elizabeth . . . did she change at all?"

" She's as like me as two peas."

" Life can be cruel," said Sir Thomas.

*   *   *

Margaret would like to have seen Gavin Johnson again for a long talk, but apart from a glimpse of his tall figure as he strode across the courtyard at Balgennan, and leapt on to his horse, she saw nothing of him until the Thursday evening before her marriage was due to take place .

She was gradually learning that her Uncle, the Earl, was one of the more important nobles in the land, and had been admitted to the King's Privy Council, which was only made up of a handful of nobles, bishops and abbots. Only the wiser men were supposed to be invited to join this Council, and matters discussed there were kept secret, then either forgotten or passed on to Parliament for general discussion. A meeting of this Council had only recently been held.

"How long before our good King stab thee in the back, sir?" Archibald had taunted. "Another summons, I jaloose, to be closeted with His Majesty and plot the ruin of all of us, or did I mistake the King's Messenger riding in this very morn?"

"Hold thy wheesht, boy," his father thundered. "Is this the thanks I get for giving thee an education? You have been sent to Paris to be taught at the Bishop of Moray's College, and there I stood in error. If I had put you to our new St. Andrew's, maybe you would have been less careless of manners and had more respect for thy betters. Instead you are cavorting with riff-raff like the Grahams and the Stewarts."

Margaret, listening, looked again at Sir Archibald. She could not imagine him learning gentleness and respect, yet her first impression of brutish behaviour and uncouth manners was beginning to pass, and she suspected that a lot of it had been put on for her benefit. Sir Archibald saw that she was not turning a hair, neither was she turning up her nose when he deliberately tried to shock and disgust her by rude manners such as demanding his pot before she was out of the room, and laughing loudly when she hurried the faster to the door.

"Thy modesty will ill become thee, Mistress, after Friday," he yelled, and she had gone to her room and stood there, overcoming her revulsion, then firming her mouth. Archibald did not want the match. She was beginning to feel sure of that. She had taken to sitting in his sick room, feeling that they must get used to one another before the knot was tied, and for the first day she almost tried to seek out Gavin Johnson and plead with him to return her and Sarah to Wrykin Hall. But suddenly Archibald had grown tired, and lay back after a tussle with the manservant who would glance with a wooden look at Margaret now and again, yet without signs of complaint against his master.

" There is a game called Chess, Mistress," Archibald said in a surprisingly quiet voice. " Do you know the game?"

" I have played it with my father, but alas his skill was greater than mine."

" We are pawns, you and I. We obey the Laws. But our day will come when we make the Laws. For you . . . for you it may be too late. Your decision has been made hastily, Mistress Margaret, to take thy sister's legacy."

She forced back tears. Was he now playing on her emotions? What manner of man was he, that he could be so cruel? Yet she was no longer living for her own well-being, but was consumed with desire to avenge her sister.

She stood up and deliberately went to the small narrow window of the castle, looking out across the waves which were now in a wild mood.

" Does anyone live on the rock they call Ailsa Craig?" she asked.

" It is for the pleasure of our holidays," Archibald said, grinning. " Perhaps when my wounds heal, we will spend a holiday there, so that you will get to know your husband full well."

She looked at him coolly.

" A pleasure to come, Sir Archibald."

But now he was taunting his father over some sort of matter which concerned the King and Sir Thomas was trying to keep his temper.

" Will we be honoured enough by your presence when I wed Mistress Margaret on Friday?" he asked. " Will you have the pleasure of seeing her decked out in the finery of her wedding gown, and me in my clean nightgown with my bib removed? Or does the King's business come first?"

" The King's Command is always one to be obeyed by a loyal servant," said Sir Thomas sternly, " but the messenger brought papers for my eyes alone, so hold thy tongue, boy, or I might forget your manhood and your wounds and have thee whipped. Do not forget that your own Barony is but a small addition to Balgennan, as small as Nithrie belonging to my own Squire."

He paused and there was silence in the room.

" I am still Earl of Balgennan while there is breath in my body, and while there is breath in my body, I will see that thy thinking bears better fruit. Do not heed the treasonous tales of the Grahams and Stewarts. My own youth was spent in a lawless land with King Robert who had to have his kingdom ruled for him with much jealousy and quarrelling."

He turned to Margaret. " These are sombre words and deeds for your entertainment, Mistress. I had hoped to settle thee into Balgennan with joy and merriment before your duties take up most of your time."

" Find our dear Master Gavin to escort her to the next Fayre," said Archibald. " I'm sure he has no objection and is no pretty fellow though he looks like one."

" The Squire does not deserve thy foul tongue, boy. Nor thy bride. We excuse thee because of pain. A wounded dog is always like to bite."

He turned to Margaret.

" The Squire has been given leave to see his parents at Nithrie, a small Barony southwards into Galloway. If he should earn his spurs, then Sir Gavin will have a bigger Barony bestowed on him by the King, and I pray he will be a good friend and neighbour to Balgennan."

" We will ever be enemies," said Archibald, " if he is praised much more to my detriment."

Getting up, Sir Thomas strode out of the room.

On the eve before her wedding, Margaret made her way for the first time outside the courtyard of the Castle. It had been strongly built with thick stone walls, four storeys high, the walls containing many small rooms including garderobes. The kitchen quarters were good, with storage rooms, a bakery, cellars and a well, but it was no elegant building after Wrykin Hall. Margaret had been entertained in the homes of merchants near to her own birthplace, and their houses were furnished with more comfort and elegance than Balgennan in spite of the position the Earl held in the land, yet it had a dignity and grandeur all its own.

Margaret reminded herself that there had been no mistress in Balgennan since the Countess died when Sir Archibald was a boy of ten, and wondered why the Earl had not sought a new wife. She had ventured to ask Archibald, whose lip had curled a little, then his eyes dulled.

"Like our liege Lord, he though my mother his milk-white dove. She was fair of face and had light golden hair. There is nothing of her in myself but her blood, Mistress. It grieves him that I inherited none of her beauty or grace . . . or wisdom, according to his lights. He grows weary with me when he sees no reflection of her in my uncouth face and the ugliness he finds in me."

"Do not talk so!" said Margaret, sharply. "The Earl is grieved, only, that thy wounds are ill to heal."

"He would as lief I'd died of them," said Archibald, morosely, and Margaret swung away from the window with impatience.

"I see great pity in thee . . . for thyself, Sir Archibald."

She had spent less time in his sick room, but had gone downstairs and wrapped a cloak round her shoulders. When she became Mistress of Balgennan, she would see that the servants cleaned the cobbles to a more pleasing state. Weeds grew between them, and the dung left by the horses had been cleared but sketchily. There was a heavy warm odour of animals, mingling with the stench of kitchen slops where the servants had toppled them into the sea with poor accuracy.

Going round the side of the curtain wall, she could see a trail of rotting refuse, left to slither down the rocks, and her nose wrinkled fastidiously.

"Lazy blockheads," she thought, angrily, "taking advantage of the Earl's preoccupation with more important matters, and the Squire's absence." Though Gavin's duties were to serve his master, and not to worry himself about household affairs.

Thinking about him, she walked a little further down a cliff path, drawing her cloak closer round her gown. Wrykin Hall was fairly close to the Solway Coast, but Balgennan was washed by the Firth of Clyde which had been known to toss boats cruelly to the death of those who had embarked on the frail craft.

Margaret had caught Archibald watching her a few times with the sombre brooding look in his eyes.

" I grieve for thy disappointment," he said.

" In what am I disappointed?"

" Surely a young and beautiful maid must yearn for a knight on a silver horse to carry her away, and love her with words and the passion of flowers ... the sweetness of the rose petals and the delicacy of the lily. There will be nothing of this with me. I cannot even offer thee ... love."

She stared at him steadily.

" I ask for no love, but I ask for respect. Can it be that thy love is already given?"

He turned away and she saw that this time she had come near to a truth, if not upon it.

" Your tongue is a sad mistress," he told her. " It runs away with you. But I will not have a wife catechising me. My lord, the Earl, is already about his business in this. He would have me pour out my thoughts, every second, for his perusal."

" Because your loyalties are not his?"

" That, too, is man's work, not woman's. Do not be so enamoured of reading and writing that you must venture to put our house to rights by wisdom and advice. Your needle will be kept well plied. We maun make the best of one another and raise sons."

" My mind and thoughts will not be confined to the household."

" Then let not your thoughts trip from your tongue."

" My sister would have made you a better wife. Sweet, she is, and gentle. I cannot believe her dead."

She was watching him closely, and saw that he moved restlessly.

" She must have been wayward, too, else she would have paid heed to instructions. Your sister is dead. Do not spend your days probing her death. Keep your own health sweet."

His eyes had large black circles round them, his face white,

and she began to wonder what he looked like when he was
well and robust. Perhaps it was his ill-health which brought
out the prominent bones and made his hair dull and matted
with lack of care.

Margaret was thinking of his grey face, moistened with
sweat, as she picked her way down the cliff path to the sea,
holding out her cloak as though she would wish the lashing
waves to cleanse her of all contact with Sir Archibald Johnson.

The more she talked with him, the more she wondered if
he knew what had happened to Elizabeth. He seemed very
sure that she was dead. How could he know that for certain?

There was a noise behind her and she whirled round, ever
on the alert for beggars who were known to have few scruples,
then she relaxed, hearing that it was a horseman, and soon she
saw Gavin Johnson riding towards her.

"Are you mad, Mistress?" he asked, dismounting, and she
saw fear and anger in his eyes. "What is the meaning of
standing here alone? I did not see you attempting flight when
I came within sight. I could have been a rogue or a beggar!"

"I heard your horse. I know that a rogue would have to be
a brave fellow to ride so close to Balgennan, and a beggar
would not be riding."

"There you mistake the matter. Our beggars often ride
when their betters walk. Let me escort you away from this
path by the sea. I should have thought your sister's lesson
would be learned by thee."

Margaret stared at him.

"Then the beggars are rising from the sea and snatching
at their victims? Perhaps they are mermen or mermaids."

"It is not for amusement," he said, soberly. "I grant you
that this path is safer than most, but . . . but there are many
secrets writ in the sea."

"And in the sand, near the Inn with the kindly host."

"Aye," he said soberly.

As they neared the cobbled yard of the Castle again, they
could see servants scurrying about to obey the Earl, who had
decided that the marriage be celebrated with some ceremony
and a feast prepared for those who could eat with them at

table. The remains would be given to those who served the
estate, and the poor who lived in tumbledown turf houses
with ox hides for doors to shelter the occupants from wind
and rain. Margaret had seen a few of these hovels as she rode
north, and had shivered at the thought of living each day within
such a shelter.

Gavin slowed his step to hers, leading his horse, then he
turned to look at her, his young face handsome and ruddy with
health.

" I cannot change thy destiny nor my own, Mistress," he
said. " Sir Archibald has found himself in strange company
ere now, men who would seek to gain hold of Balgennan by
stealth and by influence, seeking to dodge past my lord, the
Earl, to his son. They breed hatred and dissent between father
and son. The King reigns wisely and well, even if his decisions
seem cruel and unjust at times. He is not averse to slicing off
the stinking limb to save the rest of the body."

" And the stinking limbs can easily make a fine stench,"
mused Margaret.

" Aye, Mistress. I knew thy head was long and thoughts
cool after the temper had gone. Would that . . . would that
your life was mine to treasure and cherish, but it is not so
and never will I speak so again. But I know thee to be woman
enough to listen, and to know, and to forget."

Margaret's heart had begun to race, knowing that Gavin's
simple honesty had made the position plain between. She had
grown to see that he was one man she could hold in her heart,
and that he had love for her in return. But many men and
women had to acknowledge their love, then hold it precious to
them even as they turned away and bound their lives to another.

" I am listening and I will not forget," she told Gavin,
facing him proudly. " I know your meaning, and . . . and I
thank thee. It warms my heart, with comfort, but my thoughts
will aways wish thee well, though I feel a coldness . . . " She
could not explain the fears she felt for his future.

" Just know that my greatest wish is to serve you. I shall
be at hand, if I am needed."

" I take that to my comfort. Goodnight . . . Gavin."

"Goodnight, Mistress. I, too, have a lily-white dove."

So, on the eve of her wedding, Margaret tried to heal her heart with tears.

The manservant had done his best to make Sir Archibald handsome and pleasing on his wedding day, but the stench of a rotting wound made Margaret hold fast to her own strength of stomach.

Sir Thomas was obviously delighted to see the knot tied, and though only a small party of witnesses were crowded into the bed-chamber while the priest said his blessings over them, downstairs several lords and their ladies had gathered to welcome the new young Mistress into their society. She wore a gown she had brought from Wrykin, of fine silk and pretty adornment of pearls and brilliants, and the ladies found it a topic of interest.

"I had a fine packman, a gay fellow," said Lady Catherine Douglas, "and willing to smuggle me a length of silk from over the Border, though it be against the law."

"And my Lady obeys the law," said the Countess of Buchan, laughing.

"I *do* obey the law, as far as it is good for my King and my Country. Though my liege is sadly lacking in feeling when it comes to a lady's dress. I have talked with the Queen who encourages his taste, but she feels that although he loves riches of adornment in his own clothes and rich hangings for Linlithgow, he has more worries in his head than adornment for the ladies, and I would not have him troubled."

When Archibald was brought down and placed near the table on a day-bed, his face pale with the effort and, Margaret suspected, the pain of his wounds, she watched him smile as the Earl toasted the King, and Lady Catherine was quick to accept the toast.

"To my bride!" cried Archibald, and Margaret was grateful to him for the merry-making and quips which followed. In spite of the coal fire, she felt cold in her silks, and could see Gavin Johnson's white face always somewhere among the crowds.

She grew tired with the merry-making, and listening for

clues as to who was in league with whom. She saw that Archibald's face was growing red with fever and excitement, and that he was drinking too much ale, and shouting to her embarrassment when she tried to influence him and have him taken back upstairs to the sick room.

" My wife would have me at work! " he cried. " Soon she might wish me weak-bodied again! "

There were great howls of laughter, and Margaret saw Gavin turning away. Then the guests were departing or being taken to their quarters for those who had ridden a distance and were staying the night.

Soon the servants and the poor were let loose on the remains of the feast, and Margaret watched for a moment while the bread was torn into small pieces and fought over savagely. It was a delicacy seldom enjoyed by the common people, even thought they ate meat and fish.

Outside in the courtyard, a bonfire was lit, and the Great Hall was cleared while they all went out dancing and singing. Archibald, drunken, was once again in his bed-chamber, and Sarah Cowan drew Margaret away and helped her up to the bridal chamber, where she was unlaced from her bridal gown and helped into a linen shift for her night attire.

The bridal bed was vast, and she did not know whether to be glad or sorry that she occupied it on her " lane," as the Earl had put it. Listening to Archibald's drunken snores nearby, she decided she was glad, and wondered if she had better make her confession on Sunday that another face was in her mind and heart on her wedding night, as she finally dropped into an exhausted sleep.

FOUR

She was the Lady Margaret Johnson, Mistress of Balgennan, but nothing seemed to have changed for her, thought Margaret, as she jabbed an embroidery needle viciously into her finger. She was no needlewoman as Elizabeth had been. Instead her ear had ever been keen to listen to the gossip of the day and to follow the rule and law of the Country, even as a boy would do.

Margaret longed for someone with whom she could discuss and argue such matters, but when she tried to give an opinion before Archibald or the Earl, she was treated with gentle indulgence. Gallantry towards the ladies was the order of a gentleman, but it left Margaret frustrated and full of irritation. Oh, had she been a man, how much she would have argued and fought, and been inspired to try to raise new spirits out of mistakes and disappointments.

Sir Archibald had given up trying to sicken and disgust her after she became his wife. It was as though that now the knot was tied, he had accepted her, but more with sullen looks than joyful ones.

Margaret had surprised the servants by appearing in the kitchens of the Castle. Sir Thomas had told her to heed not the running of the place, and Margaret had found a dark-eyed, full-blown woman in charge of the household. From her bold looks and tossing head, Margaret jaloosed that her position in the household was held through pleasing the Earl at night as well as by day.

She waited a few more days for the Earl's return, accompanied by his Squire, from a meeting of the General Council in Edinburgh. He was tired and his meat had no doubt been better prepared by good hostesses who offered him hospitality on his journey home. Margaret saw him push about his plate distastefully.

"Perhaps the sheep had grown extra sinews before it was slaughtered," he commented, "or my teeth grow weak in my mouth."

"Or the kitchen servants could spend more time at the roasting of it than the roistering with one another," said Margaret.

"What's that? Think ye my kitchen ill managed then?"

"That I do," said Margaret. "It grieves me to see it so, when thy wife must have laboured well to set it to such good store. Now the hand at the helm is a careless one, and the servants do not take kindly to supervision by one no better than themselves."

She stared directly at her father-in-law, who stared back, then grew to discomfort under her eyes.

"It is no easy task making a good household with only men to be served."

"That has changed now, my Lord Earl. I could order the household if you give me leave."

She saw a slow smile reach his eyes, then his lips.

'So you must earn thy spurs, too, Lady Margaret? Very well then. I give you leave to do as you will."

She nodded, still gazing at him levelly.

"And if the servants like it not? Or if . . . only one likes it not?"

His face grew cold and rather aloof.

"I cannot imagine that the Lady Margaret Johnson would be disobeyed under Balgennan's roof. Especially when she assures us that she can manage the servants . . . every one of them."

Her own head tossed up proudly.

"The woman servant who wishes to wear silks instead of her own homespun will find a poor gown on her back when she deals with me."

45

The Earl nodded, his eyes still cool and she felt that she might have made a mistake in taking him to task, however obliquely, for something which was, after all, his affair. Yet her own position had to be defined else she would never gain any form of serenity. Happiness was something she did not even consider. If there had been love between her and Archibald, then sooner or later she may have forgotten to seek continually for her sister, but the longer she knew Archibald, the more of a stranger he became.

Sir Thomas leaned forward on the table.

" Since our kitchens must be swept clean and a cauld wind blawn through the Castle, then let it reach into thy husband's sick room, Lady Margaret," he said, heavily. " His wounds are taking over long to heal, and the good plans laid down for wedding him with thee will be but a mockery if he lies down much longer under the poison of his sores. A guid wife is capable of putting her household in order, but she aye rules the sick room, and attends to her husband's good health herself."

Margaret's face was scarlet. The Earl had turned the tables well and truly, and she knew herself at fault. Yet she sometimes looked at Archibald and found it a nightmare that he was her spouse and as close to her in law as anyone could be.

" We maun ensure a new generation for Balgennan," said Sir Thomas with some deliberation. " The next heir is my cousin at Nithrie, father to my own Squire, though we be near of an age. I would rather my own line was carried on here at Balgennan and what better than through my sister's child?"

" My father's forebears were from Galloway," said Margaret.

" Aye, but Cumberland lands are sweeter to them. The time might come when the Border will be drawn further south again, when our King considers who has a right to it on the other side of the Solway, ourselves or young King Henry."

" My father hopes for peace and for things to be left as

46

they are," said Margaret. "England's debt is heavy and there has been much poverty through warring with France, but good county families, like my father's, are taking pains to protect their own counties and county towns."

"As are the Percies, and the Nevilles," said Sir Thomas, and Margaret bit her lip, knowing that these two families spent more time in private war than in building up wealth and trade in their own counties.

"We maun see that our own country holds fast to the General Council," said Sir Thomas. "Ach, but what am I doing here talking thus with thee, Mistress, when a young female such as yourself is better employed in her household duties. Matters o' State are men's work, and not for the petticoats. Blaw the Castle clean if ye will, but blaw nothing else into my ear. You see but one side to the story."

Again Margaret bit her lip. It was ever so. Just when she was being allowed to listen to ideas which gave her great interest and pause for thought, it would be remembered that she was a mere female, and she would be sent about her business. Some day there would be Queens in power, strong enough to rule and she doubted not that they would make as much show of it as the men.

Once when she had made that remark to Gavin Johnson, she had caught his laughing eyes on her, and there had been a gust of merriment from his lips.

"If such a Queen had thy spirit, Mistress," he had told her, "then my sword arm would be twice as strong in her defence."

The words had warmed her and warmed her now as she rose from the table. She was going to need all her courage in the new few weeks to turn Balgennan into a well-run household such as she was used to.

Before she left Sir Thomas, she paused again to ask him a question.

"I would be pleased to see the physician and discuss with him what best can be done to relieve my husband's wounds," she said. "It is now some days since you mentioned his journey to Balgennan."

"He was visiting my kinsman at Nithrie. Master Gavin's mother has been sick, but it was only a light fever, and the physician was travelling north again to see Archibald. He should be here this day, or no later than tomorrow."

Margaret sighed with relief.

"I will wait for him with no small welcome. He can teach and advise me what is best for the curing of the wounds, then I feel the fevers will also be cured. The one arises from the other. I will go and prepare fresh linen, and if you give me leave, I will change the bandages."

Sir Thomas frowned.

"Those are left to the physician lest we bleed the wound afresh."

"Sarah Cowan will help me boil herbs as a soothing unguent against the poisons. They have been used before in the cooling of wounds."

"Very well, but bear in mind the fact that I ask you to nurse your husband well, and not more ill."

"I will do my best," said Margaret.

The stench of the sick room was abominable. The doctor made regular calls, a fat middle-aged man, plump as a pigeon, who got his patients better by leaving possets and unguents, and a bracing word, which made light of their illness and encouraged them to think themselves better already.

Margaret had not thought much to his skills last time he came, but her status had now changed, and she would have him return for consultation. She took Sarah with her into Sir Archibald's room, then ordered the manservant out when she saw her husband's face greyish-white with pain, and beads of moisture on his brow under a thatch of hair matted with sweat.

"Go and bring boiled water and fresh linen," she said to Sarah. "I will see to this myself. The physician should have attended to this yesterday, but he did not arrive. Sir Thomas has given me leave . . . nay, *shamed* me into my wifely duties . . . to do what I can."

"Oh, Mistress Margaret, you have no skill in doctoring. Bessie was our skilled wife with herbs and she is with the Mistress Elizabeth . . ."

48

"Bessie Laird is not here," cried Margaret. "Do as I tell you, woman, and bring that bottle of herbal mixtures my mother placed in my pack-bag against accident on the journey. It's time I tried our own remedies, and did not depend on the physician, or that monk who brewed up medicines to get Sir Archibald better."

Sir Archibald was staring at her through pain and a touch of fever again in his eyes.

"I will have no woman touch my wounds," he cried.

"Hush, thee. I'm no 'woman', I'm thy wife," said Margaret.

"You are the woman I married from my sickbed," he told her. "No wife, nor maybe will be. I wished for no wife but Nell, but now that fiend would have them all killed . . . Nell, too . . . could he but find her. But she's hid . . . she's hid!"

The colour was rushing into his face which was becoming polished scarlet instead of grey with sweat, and Margaret glanced at Sarah. She had no idea who "Nell" was, but presumed that it was the King who was all set to dispose of her. But it was obviously the meanderings of a very sick man.

"Tell the Earl he must send out a party to seek for the physician," she bade Sarah, quickly, "then return here. We must bathe and purify these wounds. Hurry now, Sarah. Then return with the boiling water and clean linen."

A short while later the Earl came striding in, and Margaret gave him scant attention, except to give him orders to locate the physician, and to assure him that she was coping, though her knees felt like water, and there was sickness in her stomach.

"I have served thee ill," she said to Sir Thomas. "I have neglected my husband, and if you had not reminded me of my duties, his health would go ill for him at this time. But with God's help . . . and the physician's . . . we'll have his fever down again. I have seen men worse in pain and rantings and ravings when their wounds are affected by poison, but I have a medicine brewed in my mother's household which will cool the poison and draw it forth instead of healing it in, as the nursing here has been wont to do."

"There's a party of horsemen already on its way for the

physician," said Sir Thomas, but his voice grew stern. "I leave my son's good health in thy hands then, Mistress. Would . . . would you wish for help from the household?"

They were both aware of the meaning.

"I would wish for clean linen for the bed," she said, briskly. "All else can be done by Sarah and myself."

"I thank thee, Lady Margaret," said the Earl, rather gruffly. "We cannot see one another without a quarrel, but he's my son and I loved his mother. His own love was . . . foolishly placed, but that's got nought to do with thee. It has turned out well. So get him better and all will right itself."

He moved aside as Sarah Cowan returned carrying a bowl of boiling water, followed by servants carrying clean linen. The bold-eyed woman Margaret had encountered in the kitchen quarters was not among them.

*   *   *

Margaret was appalled by the first sight of her husband's naked body after stripping off his soiled linen, saturated with sweat and pus. She had gained the impression that he was a big man of heavy stature, but now she could see that although his muscles were well developed, his flesh hung on him, wasted by fevers and ill use. The wound which had ripped his left arm, then slashed down the side of his body, had grown evil-looking and made her turn away to fight down nausea.

"Go away, Mistress," panted Archibald, his fever cooling again as he feebly reached out for some covering. "This is no work for thy hands."

"Hush, Archibald. My place is here. I ask pardon that I did not come before now to tend your sores. Hold to the blanket, husband. This will be like another battle thrust."

She used the bottled herbs freely, watching him bear the pain of it bravely, her hands less gentle than her mother's or Elizabeth's would have been.

With dismay she looked at the deterioration of part of the arm wound, and her eyes darkened with fear. This was not work for semi-skilled nursing. This was work for the physician and his surgeon's instruments to cut out the neglect which could spread to poison his blood.

Quickly she bound him in clean linen ordering the servants sharply to clean the bed linen and stoke up the fire in the bedroom.

Gavin had just ridden into the courtyard and she ran down the broad steps, delighted that the physician must surely now be with him. But Gavin looked grim-faced and ill-tempered when she showed her anxiety that the man had not arrived with them.

"Is he not already here?" asked the Squire. "He must have been delayed or diverted aside when he left Nithrie. My mother has been ill of a chill and the rheumatics, but she is better this past day or two . . ."

"Sir Archibald has poisonous wounds," said Margaret. "We must have the man here to lance the wound. It needs the surgeon's knife instead of my herbs and possets. Will you return and trace the physician's route, and tell him he is needed? He may think Sir Archibald almost better by now, but the dirt of Balgennan has penetrated the wound. 'Tis time I managed the household to better standards, though this is no help for Sir Archibald. Already there is fever in him, and his tongue grows loose with his ravings."

Gavin glanced at her keenly, then turned to look thoughtfully towards the South, so that Margaret grew impatient.

"If you are afeared Sir Thomas may be put about by your absence, then I tell you, he is in a grave humour. Bring the physician, Squire Gavin, as quickly as you can find him."

He turned back to look at her, then nodded.

"So be it."

It was two hours later when Gavin returned and escorted a strange-looking scrawny man with a bright burning light in his eyes up to the bedroom, as though he were smuggling him into the house.

"But . . . but the physician?" began Margaret, and Gavin gripped her arm.

"There is no time. The physician has been delayed, but Master Paul Crawar, here, will heal Sir Archibald . . ."

" With God's help," said the man, in a ringing voice, so that Gavin looked round warily.

" Keep thy voice down, man. Thee knows the clergy are after thy blood already. If it be known that I brought thee to Balgennan . . ."

The gaunt man looked at Gavin contemptuously.

" Should I deny what I am? Or is it thine own skin which is precious to thee? But this is no time for quarrel. This man is sick. I see that his good nurse has bound his wounds clean and well . . ."

" Here is the decayed wound, sir," said Margaret, pulling aside the pad she had made. " It . . . I do not like its looks."

" Nor I, my Lady. But I've dealt with worse and got my sick friends better with the help of God and a good nurse. Do you believe in God, my Lady, or the bleatings of his poor servants in the Church, unworthy people to preach His true love and virtue?"

" Have done with preaching," said Gavin, swiftly. " Do thy work, Master Crawar, then let me return thee to where I found thee, richer in pocket. My master, Sir Thomas, will be generous even if he does not approve of the doctrines learned in foreign parts."

" I've found many who listened to James Resby on my travels," said Paul Crawar. " In Bohemia, it is easy for people to listen to the doctrines of the great Wycliffe . . ."

" Hush thee! The King hates heretics. Resby paid for his power and influence with his life."

" What is Life if it cannot be lived by the things we believe to be true and good?" asked Crawar, scornfully.

He had taken out a roll of instruments and was drawing a thin shining blade through a candle flame, then motioning Margaret to hold her husband's head. Archibald was mumbling and she was not at all sure how much he realised what was happening to him.

Then he screamed and stiffened in her arms, and she held on to him while Gavin grasped his legs, and Sarah Cowan had to help with a bowl of hot water and clean linen for the wound.

" I'll give you something to physic him with," said Crawar.

" A posset to soothe, and keep the wound clean and in good heart. If it be the will of God, he will live to fight again, no doubt, and despatch other Children of God in bloody battle."

" Who are thee?"

The words dropped like stones around them, and turning, Margaret saw the Earl framed in the doorway and Gavin's colour change to sickly grey. Only the man, Paul Crawar, was unperturbed as he ran his medical instruments along the flame and washed his hands with hot water before going over to look down at Archibald who had dropped off to sleep, his breathing easier.

Margaret had heard enough to realise that this man was a Lollard, who was already, loved, feared, or hated as he went around preaching new doctrines against the Holy Church of Rome. The Lollards were fanatics, but whereas she had only heard of those who ranted and raved, this man had put his powers into healing.

She ran forward to the Earl.

" The physician had been diverted somewhere else and has not turned up in time," she said, hurriedly. " This excellent gentleman has done his work for him, and done it better, if I may be bold enough to say so. He deserves our thanks, my Lord. My . . . my husband will get well now. I no longer feel the heaviness of his sickness in my heart. There is new hope within me."

" What say you to this, Gavin," the Earl asked, sternly.

" I knew not what to do, my Lord," said Gavin. " I had to find a physician . . . Mistress . . . Lady Margaret bade me, and I knew the doctor has . . . has not been seen this two days."

" Not been seen?"

Gavin swallowed. " No, Sir Thomas. He was riding with two other men, but near the coast . . . he was last seen near the coast . . ."

Sir Thomas was very white.

" Does the household know this man is under my roof?"

" No, Sir Thomas."

" Then keep it that way. As for you, Sir, you are my guest

and must be treated as such, besides my deference being offered to thy skill in helping my son. Come to my room where I will offer you hospitality and payment, then I must ask you to leave. Thy doctrines are not mine!"

" Only because thine ears are deaf to . . ."

" Silence, Sir! My ears are deaf to nothing, nor mine eyes. I serve my King and his beliefs are mine. But I will protect thee while in my home, though I know there are those already wishful to try thee for crimes against the Church."

" Is not Evil already afoot in thy country? I would cut out Evil, even as I have cut out the Evil in thy son's body."

"You are mortal, Sir," said Sir Thomas. " Do not claim perfection in your beliefs. My own are yet mortal, too, and as such have sinful men as well as pure administering them. But they have served me well, and will serve me until death. I will not have thee babbling thy humours under my roof, but I offer thee rest, hospitality and reward before you leave Balgennan."

Margaret watched them descend the spiral stairs to Sir Thomas's room, then turned to Archibald, whose breathing was more regular. Sarah Cowan was walking about, wraith-like, in spite of her normal heavy tread, as she tidied the room and burned the old dressings.

" I thank you, Sarah, for your help."

Sarah knelt and made the sign of the cross.

" That stranger . . . he is a heretic, Mistress Margaret. 'Fore God he will roast and may end up in Hell. And the good doctor has . . . has been spirited away, just like Mistress Elizabeth, before he could treat Sir Archibald."

Margaret nodded, the cold feeling again welling up inside her body, so that she shivered. What was this Evil which removed people as though they had never been, and left no trace but the footprints of a child, and a splash of blood? It was easy to guess that the doctor's last whereabouts had been in the same vicinity as her sister's.

The cold seemed to increase so that she went to the fire and bade Sarah order more fuel. Yet no amount of heat in the room seemed to warm her through and through. Nor could she feel anything but gratitude towards the gaunt stranger, Paul Crawar, who was a heretic, yet who spent his days bringing life and hope to sick bodies.

Yet she shared Sarah's fears for his future.

FIVE

Slowly Sir Archibald began to recover his strength and as Margaret nursed him, he grew more and more silent towards her. At times she thought she would have preferred his noisy brashness. Instead he thanked her quietly for her ministrations.

Gavin also went quietly about his business and spent long hours in the armoury, cleaning his master's weapons, then checking the weapons of the servants and the men living on the estate, according to their rank. He caught boys playing football and boxed their ears, with secret sympathy.

" A few blows might give thee better hearing," he told the chastened boys. " Did ye not listen to the good Town Crier reading new laws? Are you so well lined in the pocket that you can pay fourpence fines for playing football instead of practising with your bows and arrows? Does it please thee that some English boy is ere now as swift and true as the best of his father's men, and will make pin cushions of all of you should we be called upon to defend our good Earl from a raid?"

The boys said nothing, scuffing their feet in shoes hardly fitted for playing their favourite game. Gavin fished surreptitiously into the pocket of his coat for sweetmeats.

" My brains are soft as butter," he told them, " that I should remind you of lessons learned by feeding you sweetmeats instead of whipping thy buttocks. Back to school tomorrow and learn thy letters, all of you."

" Aye, Sir Squire."

Gavin recognised the cheeky grin of the dominie's eldest boy and thought that a word to his father would result in a thrashing from an arm of no small experience.

Yet the dominie had plenty of learning in his head, and had once been sent as a Wise Man to Parliament by the Earl, to speak for him in local affairs. It was a great honour, and he was now well respected by the local people. Gavin's eyes were thoughtful as he sent the boys about their business, and he wondered if a word in the dominie's ear about a different matter might not come amiss.

The man, Paul Crawar, was an exceeding embarrassment to him, and he could do with a man of education and discretion to talk to the Lollard, and get him out of the country before the clergy began to notice that his teachings were gathering more attention than their own.

Had it not been for the man's skill in curing Sir Archibald of his wounds, the Earl would have had little hesitation in clapping the man in gaol, but as it was, he had been allowed to go about his business, though that had taken him no further than Nithrie!

Gavin had once heard the dominie speak of the first heretic to reach the district, James Resby, who had been expert at preaching the doctrines of Wycliffe, and claiming that the Pope was far from as Holy as the Church would have him be, and that no one who was not truly Holy should be Pope. It had been the dominie's opinion that the ears which had listened to, and absorbed, the teachings were like ears of corn which had fallen on fertile soil.

Paul Crawar had even greater influence in that he could lance boils and physic a fever, and Gavin's mother had been beholden to him for helping her own rheumatism and for binding up the arm of his younger brother when he fell out of a tree while crow-shooting. Gavin was perhaps going to find himself squatting the thorny hedge of divided loyalties unless he could get a long-headed fellow to speak to Crawar and encourage him to depart for Bohemia, from whence he came, his head stuffed with notions likely to lose it for him.

Men like Paul Crawar were a great nuisance, thought Gavin, in that they were beyond the run of common men and attracted admiration, however reluctant. He would rant about the original teachings of Christ, and of what sinful men had

57

made of them, his eyes flashing as though candles had been lit in his head, then the flame would be extinguished and he would clap a strong slender hand on the shoulder.

"Listen to that, Master Squire. It's a whaup. See yonder the curve of its wings against the sky. See here . . . rein in thy mount and look up at the blue of the sky through the fresh green leaves. Does not the beauty of God's earth make you wish to breathe it into men's souls? Yet what do they learn about God from men who have sworn to have compassion on the sick and succour the poor? They spend their days gathering riches when the riches should lie in the Spirit of Man."

Gavin had not known whether to be annoyed or to succumb to the liking and respect he secretly felt for the man. Paul Crawar and the Earl of Balgennan could not be more different in outlook and ideals and he hoped he would never have to choose between them one day.

In order to hurry Crawar away from the Earl's beetling brows, Gavin had bid him ride to Nithrie for succour and shelter before embarking on a journey which, he hoped, would quietly remove the physician to a place of safety.

But now the Lady Margaret was showing great interest in the man and trying to stir up similar interest in Sir Archibald.

"Do you not know where the physician has gone?" she asked. "I feel considerable unease within me when I consider that our local physician seems to have disappeared, and that the visiting stranger has also left the vicinity. What do you think would happen should a servant girl drop her pot of broth over her arms, or one of the henchmen break his head while falling from his horse?"

"We have our auld wives well versed in herbal medicines," he told her curtly, "and if a henchman be stupid enough to fall from his horse on to his head, then his ale be thrown in his face instead of being poured into his stomach. Forget the physician Crawar, Mistress. We managed before he came, and we will manage once more now that he has gone."

Now that Sir Archibald was slowly gaining strength, Gavin could see other pressing problems ahead. The Lady Margaret was wishful to visit one or two friends she had made, as she had been used to doing from her home in Cumberland. There she had travelled as far abroad as Cockermouth, Isell or even Brougham, when there were celebrations among families because of marriages, or sympathies to be carried in days of bereavement.

Now she had met the Lady Jane Kennedy from the small Barony of Greenan near the Royal Burgh of Ayr. She knew that Sir Thomas would frown on her absence from Balgennan while Sir Archibald was still convalescing, but a day's ride may be managed, especially since she was wishful to make purchases in the town.

"It will have to wait until after the Wolf Hunt," he told her. "You will have business enough in the kitchens on the day of the Hunt because Sir Thomas gives hospitality to his neighbouring barons and all the farmers and their labourers on the day of the Hunt."

"This has not been mentioned to me," pouted Margaret.

"Did I not hear Sir Thomas talk of the Hunt only last evening?" asked Gavin.

"That is so," she conceded, "but that it be a *Wolf* Hunt, not so. Nor that the kitchens must be busy. I would find me a new servant, Gavin, now that the woman servant, Janet Armstrong, who dared to laugh in my face, has gone with her baggage on a pony back to her hovel."

"She should have been whipped for insolence," said Gavin, uneasily. "She is brazen and could be a witch. She hated Sir Archibald, and his wounds grew putrid while she was under this roof. She had a web of enchantment round Sir Thomas which was torn from his eyes by yourself, so that he saw the woman for what she was, but she should have been beaten to reduce her spirit which grows like a blown-up toad. Eat no food, Lady Margaret, unless the taster says it is good, and drink no ale or water unless it first be drunk by the taster. She might try to harm you. Guard thy hair and even the parings from your fingernails or toenails as soon as they are cut. I have your well-being in my care, and I lack ease over your good health."

59

She looked away. Her own warm blood was roused by the Squire. She felt frustrated that she was still wife, but no wife, though she was now mistress of the Castle, and already she found it a sweeter place to live in.

" My health has improved ten-fold with the freshness of new brooms and water swillings," she said, " and the recovery of my husband. If you must plan a Wolf Hunt instead of supplying escort for me, then I maun go and speak with Sir Archibald."

She paused and looked back over her shoulder.

" I have not seen, nor yet heard a wolf since coming to Balgennan."

" Oh, they are still in the forests aplenty, though I suspect some labourers of encouraging their breeding within trapped land so that they may earn themselves the twopence for each whelp's head. Some of the farmers grow lax, though, and pay their fine instead of turning out to hunt like honest men. They grow rich that they can throw away a sheep in this way, but they expect the rest of us to clear the wolves who would savage their herds."

" When is the Wolf Hunt?"

" A sennight. My notion is that Sir Thomas will talk about this with you over your meal in the evening, and was only waiting till Sir Archibald was well enough to sit at table. It should cheer thy husband. He was ever keen on the kill."

She shivered. She was reminded of the violence which, she felt, was just under the surface with Sir Archibald. He was as calm as a summer day, but she felt the lowering clouds gather on the horizon, especially when Sir Thomas rubbed his hands at Sir Archibald's returning strength and wished him well enough to be " about his business." At first Margaret had not understood, but her cheeks had coloured when she saw his brooding eyes turned on her.

She went straight from talking to Gavin in the armoury to the sickroom where Archibald now lay on a day bed. Margaret had grown used to his looks which were less brutal now that the fevers had left him, and which, she saw, gave him a strong face, if ugly. She could see Sir Thomas' father in him, from the portrait which hung above the wine cupboard in the Great Hall, and which had been painted in Italy where he had travelled as an envoy for the King. Sir Thomas' own face was of noble cast with broad brow and fine eyes, and great strength to jaw-line.

"Squire Gavin tells me there is to be a Wolf Hunt this sennight," she said, taking her place on a chair beside him.

He moved his legs, then sat up straighter.

"Last Wolf Hunt raised three," he said, proudly. "The packs grow small now. By the next generation, if we cease not to punish the labourers from encouraging their breeding against a steady income from whelps' heads, they may be exterminated and one day our country will be freed of the vermin."

"I care not to see the whelps' heads," said Margaret, shuddering.

"A poor wife were you afraid to kill a chicken against starvation."

She saw a glint of amusement in his eyes and was strangely pleased that he seemed better.

"The Earl desires you to be at table for supper if thy strength is equal to the task."

He frowned again. Sometimes his "strength" relied a great deal on his mood.

"I will eat at table," he said, eventually. "My strength is up to it. Soon it will be up to other things as well and we maun have talk of it, Lady Margaret. There are things we maun discuss."

"I shall listen . . . gladly."

"I think there is liking and respect between us, but no love as between man and wife. Are these thy feelings as well, Lady Margaret?"

She was silent, looking at his white face where the drawn lines were beginning to soften. She thought of Gavin and his handsome face and glowing health, yet she knew she had compassion for Archibald.

"I can see it in your eyes," he assured her. "I have known since the beginning that your woman's love was not for me. I tried to make you turn about, but I watched you hold to thy word, and keep the bargain. Why did you come here at all? The bargain would not have been enforced after the Mistress Elizabeth . . . after her party was no more seen."

Margaret spoke as honestly as he.

" I was wounded by my sister's death . . . for I know that she is dead . . . and I wanted vengeance, and I meant to find out where the responsibility lay, and to punish the wicked were it to cost me my life. I . . . I blamed everyone I met . . . Squire Gavin, thyself, the Innkeeper and his wife in the interest of robbery, and any likely-looking wench I could find who could be jealous. But I know the crime is not at thy door, nor Sir Thomas', nor Squire Gavin's. Yet still I must find her murderer, or never sleep in my bed in the night. Do you not know who was responsible, Sir Archibald?"

His eyes had flickered for a moment when she mentioned a jealous female, and she thought of the bold insolent woman whom she had found running the household. Did the solution lie in that witch?

" I know nought," said Sir Archibald sullenly. " Many travellers have vanished against all trace if they ventured too near the shore. We have waited packmen and guests with their servants, and freemen and burgesses, in vain. Some were diverted and will come some other time, but some we will not see again."

" Cannot Sir Thomas send a party of men to investigate, to see the spot where my sister was last known to have been?" asked Margaret.

Archibald lay back, considering her from lowered brows.

" Once he headed a party of men and they searched the area in daylight and in the gloaming, though the men were full of unease towards darkness. But although some of the men could feel the evil all round them after nightfall, and felt the Devil's touch, which sets hairs to rise on the back of the neck, they did not find anything amiss. No creature molested them, and no travellers walked before them, and were swallowed up."

" What about the rock they call Ailsa Craig? Would not prisoners be kept there?"

" Aye, that is so," said Archibald, " but only prisoners against King and Country until trial is arranged. They are men who would grow powerful if unchecked."

" Then you would defend His Majesty, James First?"

Archibald's brows glowered again.

" The House of Balgennan is pledged to defend His Majesty. We have had good Kings and worthless Kings guiding and defending our Realm. My father believes that James is as good as we have ever had, and condones the methods he uses to bring unity from all parts of the Kingdom. I have questioned this and have thought the King a tyrant . . ."

His voice trailed off.

" But now your thoughts are changing?" asked Margaret, and she saw that he was gazing far out to sea, his thoughts seemingly miles away, then he sighed.

" I know not. Lying here, with past deeds history and present deeds unknown to me, I know not. But for one deed my heart will never be reconciled. Some day I will tell you, but not now."

She would like to have talked more. It was the first time he had discussed so much, and she longed to know what had gone before to bring bitterness to his eyes, and open defiance at times with his father, when his Earldom was pledged to be loyal to the Crown.

" Shall I bid the servant help you to your place at the table?" she asked.

He nodded.

" Aye indeed. 'Tis time I were my own man again, and not playing the invalid."

He smiled, one of his rare genuine smiles.

" I like thee, my Lady Margaret. I like thee very much."

SIX

That evening at dinner Sir Thomas was silent and pre-occupied after signifying his approval of Sir Archibald's presence at the table.

"Eat your meat but be sparing with the ale," he advised. "Your body has lost a portion of its flesh, but we maun build it up with good strong meat to make good flesh and not strong ale to dizzy thy head."

"Aye, my Lord. I heard thee," said Archibald.

"Is your strength likely to be fit, in a short time, for more than a seat to sit on, and to behold the waves of the ocean?" the Earl asked, and Archibald looked brighter than Margaret had ever seen him.

"Aye, Sir, be it a Wolf Hunt, you mean. Given two good henchmen to my aid, I could sit horse and raise the pack."

"Oh, aye, the Wolf Hunt," said Sir Thomas, absently. "I thought nought o' the Wolf Hunt. His Majesty was wishful to gather some friends round him, and I would have you and the Lady Margaret take your places as Heir to Balgennan."

Archibald looked cast down.

"A journey to Holyrood would maybe go ill with me," he muttered, and his father's brows puckered.

"Yet it would be less strenuous, though I have no doubt less to thy liking than raising wolves."

"The King has a wheen o' friends and nobles without the Lady Margaret and me."

"And how is Lady Margaret going to take her place among the ladies if ye do not take her to Court?" his father demanded. ' She is not the wife to shame thee by her ugliness, is she?"

Archibald regarded his wife unhappily, then turned his gaze on his father.

" I would not wish to deprive the Lady Margaret of her rightful place. When would you wish us to make the journey?"

The Earl sat brooding silently for a while.

" You might as well be told now as later, that the Lord of the Isles is showing his arrogance again, and there is unease at Court."

" His Majesty used his usual methods of bringing them to heel," observed Archibald drily, glancing at Margaret. " He sent word for all the Chiefs to come to a meeting at Inverness, and when they came he clapped the lot of them into gaol."

" He did it to show that he wanted obedience to the Crown," said Sir Thomas grimly. " What kind of obedience had the King from his Highland Chiefs? Anyway, it was your hero, Albany, who started all the trouble years ago when he gave the Earldom of Ross to his own son, instead of to the Lord of the Isles who deserved it more, and it was fought out at Harlaw. That was the first Duke of Albany for you. You might think though, that the Highlands would have learned their lesson, especially since the King dealt very firmly with Albany's family as well . . ."

" Very firmly. He only wiped the family out . . . nearly," cried Archibald, then bit his lip as though he had said too much.

" They murdered themselves when one of Murdoch's sons collected a band o' brigands about him, and set out to burn the towns, against his father and brothers being in gaol. He murdered far more folk by burning than the King. What kind o' justice would the King have meted out, if he had not brought that family to trial?"

" Some trial!'

" They were tried by good men and true and brought to justice. Didn't they deserve it for murdering the King's older brother, David, to keep the Crown off his head? James is just making certain it stays on his! James only seeks to show who

C

rules the land, that's all. He clapped the Lord of the Isles in gaol, aye, but he let him go when he felt he had learned his lesson, he and the other Chiefs of the Hebrides."

"His lesson is that he maun distrust a King."

"His lesson is that he maun *obey* his King. I declare thine own head sits in a frail state upon thy body with the treason that drops from thy lips. Remember the words might be heeded the greater, if they are spoken outside these four walls. Have a care on him, Lady Margaret. He lost his wits when he met Nell Stewart, Albany's grand-daughter."

There was a sudden uncomfortable silence, and Margaret saw that her husband's face was scarlet, and that the Earl looked as though he could have wished the words unsaid. Was this the clue, then, as to why Sir Archibald had not wanted their marriage? Was he in love with this Nell Stewart, and therefore hot-blooded in defence of her family?

"Shall I meet the Lady Nell at Court?" she asked, determined to know how she stood, and if her husband was likely to be lovesick over another female.

"No," said the Earl, gruffly, "when we say the King wiped out Albany's family, we mean just that. They are scattered and gone, their lands confiscated. My son considers it harsh justice. Perhaps he is right. But it brought the Nobles to heel, who would have spent their days trifling with the King's rulings and for the first time in years, we have a united country, and strong to withstand our enemies. Could we wish for more? Only Alexander, Lord of the Isles, dares set himself up as an equal, and goes burning Inverness, and his brave men very soon ran away and left him when the King set out to punish him for what he did. Now the upstart is once more rearing his head, and offering peace to the King. Peace! Why should he offer peace? Is he the King of England, or France, that he should start offering peace?"

Again there was a long silence.

"Is he like to come to do battle again, Sir Thomas?" asked Margaret.

"No, my daughter. That he won't do. The King has sent a message that he can come and ask for his peace. I think he will withdraw into the Hebrides, and grow sullen, but if His Majesty looks ill, then ye will know the whole of it. That is why I tell you this news, since it has just come to me by messenger."

" I shall not be strong enough in the saddle for using my sword-arm to help the King to raid the Islands," said Archibald.

Sir Thomas grew angry again, then he turned and threw some meat to the dogs.

" Rest easy. The King will not go seeking a Chieftain with little power left. You will not be called upon to fight for the King . . . and the Honour of Balgennan."

This time it was Archibald's turn to colour to the roots of his hair.

" I will aye defend the Honour of Balgennan," he said, fiercely. " Balgennan will still be here when other Kings are on the throne and the country ruled by the power of reason."

" The country *is* ruled by the power of reason. You are but a boy . . . a boy! "

The Earl looked tired and worn, and Sir Archibald's brows grew dark again.

" We will attend the King, if that be his command," he said. " I will take the Lady Margaret to Holyrood."

" Be ready to leave in two days," said the Earl. " Squire Gavin can arrange the Wolf Hunt for after our return. We attend a feast at Holyrood, on Saturday, then Divine Service on the next day, and travel back the day which follows. Make thy preparations, Lady Margaret."

" I will be ready," she said, quietly.

Secretly she was thrilled and excited to be meeting the King of Scots. The story of his captivity and the years he had spent at the English Court, had always made him seem a romantic figure in her young eyes, especially when he married the girl he fell in love with, the Lady Joan Beaufort. Margaret wanted to see the Queen who had captured a King's love.

" I maun retire," said Sir Archibald, sullenly, " if you would call the manservant, Madam."

"Rest thee well then," said his father. "The exercise and fresh air of the journey might put a rod up thy backbone."

Sir Archibald flushed, but made no answer. Margaret could not help feeling that one of the biggest drawbacks to his complete recovery was herself. She could see the Earl had similar thoughts after Sir Archibald had retired.

"Were I not ignorant of my son's nature, I wad wonder if I had bred a pretty boy," he said, sourly, and Margaret coloured.

"We are but young, Sir Thomas. The years stretch before us."

"And some of us get cut down before our prime," he said in a low voice.

"Are things well with thee, Sir Thomas?" she asked, her eyes speaking her concern.

'What is well?" he asked testily. "Aye, I'm well, as well as I can expect at my age."

Then he smiled.

"Heed me not, Lady Margaret. Do thy duty like a good lady, else my plans come to naught. Speak fair words to my son and lay the ghost of that silly child he saw once when he went a-feasting to the household of my Lord Graham, friend to the Stewarts, except for his lawful King. *He* is the one I would not trust. He has a look in his e'en when he sees his Majesty, a look I mislike. Keep Archibald away from him at Holyrood. I want him to honour our house, and not go getting in thick as thieves wi' Graham and his like."

"Very well, Sir Thomas."

"You are a fair child. I'm pleased at the way my household is run. Get thee a lady's maid if any help is needed, since the servant woman who came with you is growing old. Squire Gavin will attend to such matters. I . . . I find my kitchens are cleaner and the food more wholesome. Also the air I breathe."

He looked round at his improved surroundings.

"Nor do I miss . . . anyone . . ."

She could not mistake his meaning, and blushed a little, but already he was on to other subjects, and to telling her that she could be taken to Ayr to see the bonnet-maker, glover and shoemaker, if she so desired.

Margaret hesitated, thinking she would enjoy such an outing under proper escort, yet she had brought clothes of different quality from England, and she thought it might be amusing to be different from the Scottish ladies. There was no trade at this moment between Scottish and English merchants, so her clothing might even catch the eye of the Queen, who was English herself.

" I thank thee, Sir," she said, after a pause. " I have sufficient clothing, even for Court, as I should think."

He laughed and slapped his thigh.

" A rarity indeed! A woman who thinks of her husband's marks! Very well, Lady Margaret, but wear thy best. I want Archibald to be proud . . . as he will . . . as he will. Now, I will excuse thee."

" Aye, Sir."

" The Lord guard thy sleep."

She curtseyed and hurried upstairs, where Sarah had fallen asleep on a chair by the fireside in the bedroom. The fire had gone out, and Margaret felt out of temper with her. She *was* getting old! Maybe she ought to train up another girl. She would speak to Gavin about it after the Wolf Hunt.

* * *

Archibald's friendly mood had vanished overnight and next day he was surly and short-tempered with his manservant, and without communication when Margaret came to speak with him. She wished to know whether she was required to supervise the packing of his clothing for the journey to Edinburgh.

" Go thy way, Mistress," he told her. " I'm no peacock to strut about in fine feathers. Nor would James have it so. He grows fat with good living, or so says my Lord Graham, in spite of the sports which keep his body fit. He can out-wrestle and out-run any one of his men."

" I had heard that he plays the lute to perfection."

"Aye, that too. Mistake it not, he's a King above men."

"I think you admire him in your secret heart, husband," said Margaret, laughing to tease him from his mood.

"I would so, but I cannot forget..."

There were times when his speech became almost guttural instead of the clearer language which he had been taught abroad, and he mumbled something she could not understand.

"Tell me about Lady Nell Stewart," she invited, drawing up a chair beside him, and was surprised to see that he looked round uneasily.

"Guard thy tongue. It bodes ill to speak of her or anyone related to Albany. The King would have her put away..."

"Then she *is* alive," said Margaret, eagerly. "Did she escape her family's punishment? Is she staying with friends?"

"Wheesht, woman! I told you, guard thy tongue. There are those who would sell their grandmothers for two pence, as you must know. And even walls as thick as these of Balgennan Castle, have whispering galleries, where even a whisper can travel round and round till it finds a willing ear."

She was silent for a moment, then she jumped to her feet.

"The sea leaves the shore and we maun walk among the rocks and pick us a bowl of whelks to tempt our appetites. Come with me and show me the ones which nourish and the dog whelks which poison. I would not make a mistake, lest it be thought I would despatch thee."

Her eyes glinted roguishly, and in spite of his humour, Archibald laughed.

"Your tongue will earn you a pilgrimage to Rome."

"A pilgrimage to where the waves lap our feet, and the gulls swoop freely about our heads, is all that I ask, Sir Archibald. See, it is a fine day, and a breath of sea air will give you appetite for your meat. It is a good broth, as I can swear, since I caused the pot to be scrubbed twice-fold using a sod of clean earth, and the stock to be fresh and well seasoned before it is fit for your invalid stomach. Put on thy leathers, and leave the silks behind, and I will wear my home-spun which Sarah made for me."

They were like children as they ran about between the

huge boulders which had trapped small pools of sea-water left behind when the tide went out. Margaret had a jug, and Archibald gathered the whelks into it, showing her which ones to avoid.

" I have not had time for play for many a day," he declared, laughing.

" Why should it be so?" she asked, curiously, " In my home at Wrykin Hall, my brother played with Elizabeth . . ." Her voice still faltered on the name, but she finished with determination. " Elizabeth and me. We played a good game of tennis."

" Then you must take on His Majesty, who would make novices of us all at the game," he told her, and almost for the first time she heard him speak of his King without animosity.

" Tell me . . . no ears are behind any of these rocks . . . is the Lady Stewart still alive, and is she thy true love?"

Archibald's breath almost left him.

" Upon my word, you are an outspoken maid, I tell you. She *was* my love but we could not be betrothed. My father would have no sport with anyone from the House of Albany. Lady Helen was . . . is . . . yet a child in her ways. I could not wed with her and defy her guardians and my own before . . . before the trouble with the King. We were both but children then . . ."

" Where is she now?" pursued Margaret.

" In a poor labourer's cottage . . . near here. She lives in a turf house when once she lived in a Castle. I . . . I have been paying the servant for her keep . . . aye . . . and paying well. She never goes without meat and drink, though she maun dress like the daughter of a servant. And she does not venture to the town, even on Market Days lest a burgess sees her who has already beheld her face, and tells of her whereabouts. The King will be afeared she will whelp new enemies, as she would. She is bitter against him, Lady Margaret."

" But . . . Archibald! . . . a lady, living in such a way! She was not born to such a way of life. She maun be taken out of it, or she will be discovered, and you will be blamed, Archibald."

71

" I care not if I am blamed."

Then he looked at her, and she saw how young he was now that the flesh was beginning to cover the gaunt bones of his face. He was not nearly as ugly as she had first thought him, and no doubt the Lady Helen found him an attractive man. Margaret was not sure whether or not she liked the thought that her husband had, and would still be having, a liaison with another female.

Then the whole situation began to seem appalling.

" I care if you are blamed. Think ye that I shall enjoy the scandal of such a thing?"

" But what can I do?" he asked her, sullenly, kicking at some sea shells washed by the sand. " I hid her . . . got her away. 'Twas thought she was making for the Borders to hide in England and . . . disappeared."

" I suppose you did not hide my sister, too?" she said, bitterly.

" Mind your tongue or it is like to belong to a shrew!"

" A shrew who will ever be managing your errors to your good," she retorted.

" How?"

" I know not . . . yet," she said, still annoyed, and wanting to be very bad-tempered, though she knew it would not serve with Sir Archibald, or she would get no further information from him. " I will put it to mind, and decide what is best to do. Oh . . . Archibald! Archibald . . . look!"

She was staring with horror at something white which was beginning to stick through the sand, and Archibald bent down and pulled at it. Suddenly they were staring with horror at dismembered limbs, washed white by the sea . . . arms and legs and other unrecognisable bones.

" What . . . what is it?" she asked.

He shook his head, his face whiter than her own.

" The people . . . the travellers who have disappeared while near the coast . . . don't you see?"

" But . . . why? What is it . . . ?"

Archibald crossed himself.

" I know not. It maun be a beast o' some kind."

" A sea monster?"

" Maybe."

" Come on, let's go home," she said, taking his hand.

The Earl, watching them from a narrow window, saw them and his eyes crinkled with approval. He was examining his sword, recently cleaned by his Squire, who was getting everything ready for the journey to Edinburgh.

" It would seem that the marriage we recently attended has been well received after all."

Gavin followed his gaze, and his lips tightened, then he turned away. He had known it would come to this some time.

SEVEN

Margaret managed to find out from Archibald in which cottage he had hidden Lady Helen Stewart. The worry of having the girl near at hand, with Archibald having made himself responsible for her preyed on her mind.

" I will go and see her," she told him.

" To what purpose! " he cried. " I should not have told you. I knew it would only prod the hornet's nest, and your brain would be buzzing with the insects."

" Your brain seems to have deserted you," she returned. " Madam Nell is a Lady born. She will be quiet and still while she fears for her own skin, but soon she will wish to venture abroad. Then no one will take her for a labourer's daughter, and there are those dwelling in cots around us who would wish thee ill, I don't doubt."

" Who could wish ill on us, living on our land? We treat our people well and always have done. Men fight willingly for our House."

" What about the woman, Janet Armstrong, who controlled our kitchens to their ill? She has been returned to her hovel. Think you she won't smell out your Mistress Nell with her witchery?"

Archibald went pale.

" She would do us ill, if she could, that I grant you. I had forgotten. She had witched my father till her spell was broken by you, my lady wife. She has no cause to love either of us."

" Then let me go to see Lady Nell. Squire Gavin will take me. The Earl gave me leave to seek another woman servant to be maid to me, since Sarah grows old and slow. I will tell Gavin that a girl has been recommended who lives in that cot, and he will accompany me so that I can look at her. Then I shall find an excuse to see her alone, and tell her we will arrange her safe custody over the Border. My . . . my mother can deal with her proudly and reasonably, according to her station."

Sir Archibald drew breath and his deepset eyes regarded her with admiration. She was high-handed and autocratic, and like to push him about if he did not gain strength before she had the better of him. But for now he was grateful to her for her bold decisions which were like to solve his problems for him. He had often lain tortured, thinking of the pretty pirouetting Nell Stewart, whose impish ways had captivated him so completely.

Archibald wondered what he would have felt about King James had he not met Nell Stewart. Would he have taken his father's opinion of their rightful King, which Archibald had always considered to be blind loyalty?

Sometimes he thought he, himself, was guilty of blind loyalty towards Nell. The Lady Margaret was forcing him to see both sides of the tale. She was a determined young woman who would stand firm beside a man and it was a great temptation to lay down his load, wearily, and rest it awhile on her young shoulders.

"Leave her be," he advised. "We have no time before we depart for Edinburgh."

"We must make time," she insisted, "lest the bubble burst while we are from home. Be easy. I shall know how best to deal with Lady Nell when I see her. If she grows afraid, she will be eased. If she grows peevish, she will be reminded of her condition and, if she grows bold, she will be curbed."

"So be it," he agreed. "I give you leave to intercede. No one knows that she is in the cottage. I have not even confessed to my priest at the risk of my immortal soul."

*   *   *

The ride south along the shoreline, accompanied by Gavin, would have delighted Margaret if she had not had many things on her mind. He was well armed with a fine sword gifted by his master, after successfully defending his person against a crowd of beggars on their last trip to Edinburgh. Gavin, too, would have been happy, were it not for a fit of sulks when he learned he would remain in charge of Balgennan while the Earl and Sir Archibald, with Lady Margaret, were called to Court.

"Tarry the Wolf Hunt," Sir Thomas bade him, "a sennight, against any delay in our return. The Lady Margaret gives orders for meat to be provided from the kitchens and that will take a strong arm to supervise, lest it finds its way to labourers' stomachs long 'fore it is earned. The females work well for my Lady, but could be at the gossip when she has ridden from sight, so be ye ever alert to their waywardness and let it be known that we expect orders to be obeyed in time for our return."

"Aye, my Lord," Gavin agreed.

"See to the horses and packs, and our best men and arms to ride by our side. The Lady Margaret maun be protected when we ride beyond Balgennan boundaries and as guests of other barons."

"It will be so."

"And stop thy sulks that the Wolf Hunt be put back, or I will be obliged to make an example of you to keep the servants in good behaviour."

Gavin's drooping looks and low mood vanished. The Earl was very capable of carrying such a threat!

"I ask thy pardon, Sir Thomas. I will ever be diligent in thy service."

"Be sure that it is so," growled the Earl.

Now he was accompanying the Lady Margaret to a cot-house a few miles away to look over a labourer's daughter she had heard about. Gavin was not at all sure whence the information had come, but he presumed it was from Sir Thomas, since the Earl had bidden her train another servant.

Sometimes Sir Thomas rode around the estate with only a henchman at his side, making sure they were obeying the law by digging the required plot of land so that every man worked to make the soil more fertile, and grow more food. King James was aye concerned with feeding his people. He had seen much starvation abroad, and knew that his country would never prosper and be content unless the people were comfortable in body and belly. He demanded hard work, but gave rewards. He punished cruelty among his people if he found that some helpless creature had been ill-treated by another stronger than himself, yet he often used his own position to smite and punish.

It was only when one attended Court, and saw questions being asked, and answered, and was allowed to follow the King's reasoning, that one understood. Gavin sighed and longed a little for Archibald's position. If he had been Heir to Balgennan, how he would have cherished the title and worked hand-in-hand with the Earl to defend it. Yet Sir Archibald asked questions and tried to put himself up as the Great Judge. He was a fool, thought Gavin. The Lady Margaret had been wasted on such a foolish boy.

"See ye that rock now being covered by the tide?" she asked, beside him.

"Aye," he nodded.

"Yesterday I stood beside my husband near that rock, and we saw a fearful sight . . . bones and limbs, washed up by the sea, I wager, then part buried. Some were picked clean of flesh, some not."

Gavin turned white and reined in for a moment.

"Just near that rock, Mistress Margaret?"

"That very spot."

"So far north on the shoreline!"

He paused, and she took up his point.

"Then it is no new thing? Have you found such bones in the past?"

"Aye," he nodded, "though south of here . . . nearer to my own property in Galloway. Once . . . once it was the whole carcase of a child . . . "

She was glad of the strong sea wind blowing away the cold sickness on her face.

"Cannot a party of men band together and destroy the sea creature?"

Gavin slowly shook his head.

"We have tried to find the creature, and lie in wait for it, but its sense of danger is well developed. It only stalks the small band of travellers, and always by night, never before sundown. We maun hurry, Mistress, and get back in daylight."

Margaret nodded, and spurred her horse along the path which turned inland. The cot-house which Archibald had chosen to shelter Lady Nell Stewart was about four miles from the Castle, but it had been well chosen in its obscurity, sitting tucked behind a belt of trees, with a small stream running to the lea of it. The cotter's wife obviously used the stream to cleanse her linen, and it was now hanging on a roughly made clothes line to dry in the breeze.

It was one of the poorest built cot houses, being made of turf, with an ox-hide strung across the entrance against the humours of the weather, and as they approached, they could see the wife about to slip behind the ox-hide, pause with curiosity, then with the stillness of apprehension as she saw the two mounted figures, one a lady.

She continued to stand stiffly to attention as she recognised the Squire, and he dropped from his horse and turned to assist Lady Margaret to dismount.

"This is Lady Margaret Johnson, bride to Sir Archibald."

The two women measured one another bravely, then Margaret nodded and the cotter's wife relaxed and dropped a small curtsey in return.

"John Geddie and his wife, Elizabeth," said Gavin. "Her husband is well received by the Earl, at the Castle, and she is washerwoman when extra help is needed."

"Aye, Sir. Wi' the Lord's help."

"Wi' the Lord's help."

"The Mistress, here, would like to see thy daughter."

The woman looked alarmed, and Margaret stepped forward quickly.

"Speak with thy charge," she said, quickly, and turned to Gavin. "The girl is an orphan and in the care of good Mistress Geddie."

Again a silent message passed between them, and the woman glanced at Gavin, realising he was in ignorance of her charge's true identity, but that the Lady Margaret was not.

"She's in the hoose," she said, jerking her head. "She maun be sickly this last sennight."

"Then I shall go in and talk with her alone. I'm sure Squire Johnson will wish for a word with thy husband, and admire his good work and industry."

Mistress Geddie nodded, and led Gavin along a narrow path skirting the stream, and Margaret quickly dodged behind the ox-hide, and found herself in such poor light that she could scarcely distinguish shapes. The cotter had built his house well, though, and a fire glowed at one side of the room, which was bigger than it had first appeared. A cooking pot full of appetising soup bubbled and simmered on a swee, and nearby there was a wooden chair with the pale figure of a girl sitting on it. She wore a long plain white linen shift, but curls of burnished golden hair fell from under a linen cap.

"Who are thee?" she asked, after Margaret's eyes had become accustomed to the gloom and she had sat down and bent her gaze on the girl.

"I am the Lady Margaret Johnson, bride to Sir Archibald," she said, and the girl pulled herself into a tight knot.

"So I am to be thrown to the wolves," she said, "torn apart like my people whose only crime was to try to hold what was ours . . ."

"What was the King's," said Margaret, firmly, determined that Lady Helen Stewart knew where she stood. "Your skin is safe, thanks to Sir Archibald. He has sheltered thee well, but his worries tarded his recovery of his wounds. Now I have come to talk with you on pretence that I find a new maid-servant to serve me."

"What help can you give me?"

Margaret controlled her temper at the contempt in the girl's voice. She could see now the arrogant cast of her features, and regretted a little that she had got herself into this sorry affair. Why could not the Grahams have looked after the female since they were of such close friendship? She put this question to Lady Nell, and heard her answer contemptuously.

"Do you think I would have been hid under their roof and remained undiscovered?"

"It is dangerous for you to be hid here. Not two miles away there is the woman, Armstrong, who is full of witchery and could seek you out given the lightest whiff of a scent. She would betray you to harm Sir Thomas, now that she is thrown off like an old glove."

"We rarely see travellers. Mistress Geddie keeps her house trim and her skirts clean. She is an honest woman, but God-fearing. I . . . I grow weary though . . . weary with boredom."

"That I jaloosed. We are called to Court now, but this sennight I will be back here with plans to guide thee over the Border to Wrykin Hall, the home of my parents. My mother, sister to the Earl, will see you safe for his sake, and keep you mimsy."

The girl was silent, regarding Margaret haughtily for some time.

"So you have married Sir Archibald?"

Margaret felt she had talked enough. Captive or not, Lady Nell had lost none of her arrogance, and she was not well-mannered enough to offer thanks for help which Margaret was about to give, at risk to her own skin.

"Remain quiet," she said. "Tell the good wife I wish thee well and have no thoughts of betrayal. I would have you safe to protect my House. I shall find someone trustworthy to give you safe conduct. God be with ye."

Nell Stewart said nothing, and Margaret went back out into the sunshine, to see Gavin still deep in conversation with the cotter. Seeing her standing in the sunshine, he made his farewells, and walked with Mistress Geddie towards her.

"She is sickly this day," said Margaret. "I will see her again when I return from our visit to Court, this sennight."

"Very good, my Lady."

Margaret slipped a small purse into her hand, as she followed Gavin down the track to the broader road.

" I could find you a stronger girl among the cotters' children," said Gavin. " A sickly maid is not like to serve thee well."

" It may put the roses in her cheeks," said Margaret, carelessly. " Mistress Geddie has been spoiling her, I think."

" Spur thy horse, Mistress," said Gavin, looking round as the sky began to dull. " We maun be home before the sun slips behind the Arran mountains."

" It turns the sea to scarlet," said Margaret, watching the long scarlet fingers reaching out through the silvery-grey of the sky.

She shivered, remembering the tales of blood on the sand.

" Ride, Gavin," she cried. " My mount would stretch her legs apace! "

They said no more, but were glad to be within the courtyard of the Castle, over the drawbridge and through the yett. Margaret left Gavin to attend to the horses, and walked wearily up the steps and into the Great Hall.

EIGHT

Margaret was to remember her first visit to Edinburgh as the most exciting experience of her life. She had not realised what a powerful Nobleman her father-in-law was until they set out for the Court of King James at the head of a band of fine mounted horsemen.

The Earl and his son, Sir Archibald Johnson of the Barony of Croyan, clad in fine robes suitable for meeting and mingling with the other Nobles, looked majestic as they rode proudly forward, their standard raised, and Margaret was glad her own clothing was fine enough to bear the scrutiny of the ladies she would meet.

Archibald's clothing still hung on him, showing how much weight he had lost, but already the colour of health was in his cheeks, and his eyes were brighter. He had said little when Margaret informed him that Lady Helen Stewart was still in good health, but she was finding the cottage irksome, and Margaret would arrange to send her to Wrykin Hall as soon as possible.

"My mother will be in need of a companion," she told Archibald. "The Lady Helen will not be too proud to give her this service, I trust. With her safety secured, then your own position can best be discussed. And mine. It is no joy to me to be wife, yet no wife."

Archibald flushed.

"Neither is thy love freely given to me. But I thank thee, Lady Margaret, for ensuring safety and comfort for Nell. Her state is not to be coveted."

Margaret softened. She had not really liked Nell Stewart, but she could put herself in the young girl's place and feel sorry for her. With battles fought and lost, families were often obliged to flee their homes and go into hiding and it was part of life to accept a change in fortune. Yet the girl was young, and beautiful. Margaret had felt unaccustomed jealousy, but did not care to seek into her heart reasons for wanting the girl out of her life. That she was a threat to her own safety was enough.

The party had set out shortly after dawn and were weary unto death when they rode into Edinburgh, and to the accommodation set aside for Balgennan. To her relief, Margaret found she was being bedded in a small room with several other ladies against the limited accommodation. The Queen's Lady of the Household made no bones about an apology and the other ladies bandied words with her amidst laughter which brought the blushes to her cheek.

She was delighted to see Lady Catherine Douglas among them, and the lady came to Margaret's rescue.

" Ye poor clucking hens," she said, scornfully. " Leave the bride to her blushes. Tomorrow will be a full day with feasting and merry-making a-plenty, though we will be required to go for our worship to Holyrood Church on the Sabbath Day. Have you brought clothing enough, Lady Margaret, having lately come over the Border to marry with Balgennan? 'Tis cauld winds which blaw in Scotland, compared to the soft breezes in West Cumberland."

" That isn't so far away," protested Margaret, " and my blood is Scots, my mother being sister to the Earl. My father inherited Wrykin Hall from an uncle, though he finds it a sweet property and my brother, in his turn, will make a good steward."

" If he loses it not in a Border raid! We grow weary of seeing our lands put to the torch."

" We've had more years of peace and rest on the Borders under our King than for some years," put in the young Countess of Buchan. " Are you a loyal subject to our King James?" she asked, turning to Margaret. " Your husband has

83

been heard to make ill-considered remarks. I meant to warn you when we came to Balgennan."

"My husband rode into the town beside his father, and under his standard," said Margaret, proudly. "He will swear allegiance to His Majesty tomorrow if his loyalty be questioned."

"See, the child drops with fatigue," put in Lady Douglas. "Cease chattering and rest your bones. Your legs need strength to carry them through the morrow."

*   *   *

The Court of King James First was not as resplendent as the Court of Henry V, where he had been brought up, as Margaret knew, yet it had a simpler quality of dignity and worth which made an impression on her. She was also informed that Linlithgow Palace, which James and his Queen had furnished, was as fine as any to be found.

The King, himself, was a very impressive figure and she knew she could never give anything else but loyalty to this man, as she was led forward and presented, making a deep curtsey, while Archibald made obeisance beside her, and they received the King's blessing.

He was a very strong, athletic-looking man with the ruddy looks of good health and bright keen eyes, as he smiled at her approvingly.

"So! Thee seeks a bride from England," he said to Sir Archibald, then laughed as he turned to his Queen, a slender lady, fair as a lily, by his side. "Why, then, what is wrong with wedding an English woman? Why, only that they are stubborn and wayward, and of shrewish tempers, with sulky eyes and pouting mouths." He laughed uproariously, then caught the Queen's hand.

"Nay, we find ourselves a lily-white dove, Sir Archibald. It is well done."

"It is well done, Your Majesty," said Sir Archibald and for a moment his eyes met Margaret's and she could only see merriment there, and a warmth which indicated that the King could captivate. She found herself wishing that this state of affairs could last, then blushed as they stepped aside to make way for another Baron and his lady. It might have pleased her to grow soft towards her husband, if his feelings for her were the same, but the Lady Nell Stewart stood between them.

Margaret almost felt faint when she remembered, and wondered what the King would say if he knew that they were giving succour to the daughter of the House of Murdoch, Duke of Albany, whom he had hated.

Now the King was greeting Sir Robert Graham and his lady, and Margaret was suddenly aware of a silence in the large company of courtiers, nobles, bishops, burgesses and wealthy merchants who were gathered together for a feast of merrymaking such as James loved now and again.

It was plain, however, that there was little love lost between Sir Robert and his King. Archibald had told Margaret that Sir Robert had been one of the first Nobles to fall victim to the King's wrath when he defied him over a matter of law shortly after James began to reign, and he had ended up in prison. More recently, Sir Robert's favourite nephew had also challenged the King's rule, and had been lucky to escape with his life, his lands now being in the hands of the King.

It was a battle of wills, as the strong arrogant Nobleman faced his King, yet dared to challenge his rule. Suddenly Margaret could see why the Earl admired a strong King, and how difficult it would be to keep powerful Barons in harmony with one another, and working together for the good of the Realm, without hitting strongly, and hitting hard at those who questioned authority, and refused to obey the laws agreed by Parliament or the General Council. Yet even as the thoughts went through her mind, she was aware of Archibald's tension, as he stood beside her. She knew he admired Sir Robert Graham, and she wanted to pull him away and rip the wool from his eyes.

" See ye not," she wanted to say, " that he is arrogant and challenging in his arrogance. See how his Lady stares boldly at the Queen! "

" So! " cried James. " We bid thee welcome, Sir Robert, if

thee come with softness and harmony in thy heart. We would have thee merry, Sir, as merry as the Master of Unreason. We trust you will not cool our meat at the feast with disapproval of our rule."

"We hope the Crown sits comfortably on thy head, Majesty," said Sir Robert, bowing, "and that thy body be strong enough to keep the weight of it from toppling. As to the feast, I am ever ready for my meat. It lends strength to my sword-arm."

"We trust thee will be circumspect with thy strength," said the King and nodded to Lady Graham who seemed to have difficulty with her curtsey. Margaret's eyes met those of the Queen and she saw that she looked pale and strained. Suddenly she was experiencing the strange icy feeling again, which had come upon her when Elizabeth disappeared, and she could scarcely prevent a shiver from passing through her body.

"Your garments are soft and fine for the winds which blaw cold," said Archibald beside her. " Soon we will take our place at the table for the feast and you will find warmth from the torches and the dishes."

"The cold is in my heart," she whispered. " I trust not Sir Robert Graham and his lady."

His face grew dark.

"He is ever noble and ever proud and brave for his rights. Is it well that we should be meek in the face of injustice?"

"If it *is* injustice," Margaret agreed. " But were I to choose then my loyalty lies with our lawful King, and with the Earl who has sworn allegiance. Is thine own allegiance forsworn?"

Sir Archibald's face coloured even more.

"Guard thy tongue, Lady Margaret. There are ears which may be keen to overhear. I *have* sworn allegiance. I stand by it."

Margaret gave him a radiant smile.

"That pleases me, Archibald. This is a time of merry-making and feasting, the first time I have been called to Court since our marriage. Cannot we enjoy the festivities along with the Earl, thy father, who has now the King's ear? My eyes tell me he is one of the King's favourite nobles, and one to trust. I see the Queen, too, is relaxed and smiling in his presence."

Archibald nodded, then had a last whispered word.

" If there is a spectre at the feast, it will be Duke Murdoch and his family. Nell Stewart should be here to take her place with the ladies."

Now it was Margaret's turn to frown, and to look round hastily, though the chattering throng was busy with gossip and laughter.

Suddenly she was aware of eyes following her, and she turned to stare at the strange-looking gentleman whom the King had already presented to the Court as a visitor from Italy, Aeneas Sylvius Piccolomini. Margaret had remembered the name, even as she remembered the man, and now she could see that he was looking at her with ill-concealed admiration, and she could not keep the roguish look of devilment from creeping into her eyes. Archibald may hanker after Lady Helen, but it was nice to see that one man found her attractive, though she suspected that Aeneas Sylvius might find most ladies agreeable to him. She watched him limp forward, and bow over her hand.

" I see you are not a lady native to the country," he told her.

" How so, Sir?"

" Your gown, my Lady. It is of fashionable cut."

" Not quite such high fashion now, Sir," she laughed, then looked concerned when she saw him limping again as he drew her aside for conversation.

" I trust you have not been injured, my lord Piccolomini."

" Rheumatism, my Lady, brought on by a vow I made when I thought I would perish before reaching these shores. Our ship was tossed and turned by gales and high winds, and I vowed I would walk barefoot to the nearest Church and give thanks to God for safe deliverance, should He see fit to spare one of His servants. Our ship landed at North Berwick, but in your barbarous country, I had to walk six miles barefoot, on frozen ground, to Whitekirk. My feet have paid the price."

She had difficulty in following his Italian-accented dialect, but listened avidly, her eyes alight with fun. She missed the light humours and wit of the society she had left behind at Wrykin.

"Then you find our land little to thy liking, Sir?" she asked, laughing.

"Ah, it is droll, very droll. Your palaces are austere, plainer than the homes of merchants in my own country, and so cold. Ah, how cold they are! And so bare. Where are your pictures, your paintings, your Art?"

"Art? Is Art so important in your own country?"

"Some day you will come to Italy, and see what a rich and beautiful country it is, such as you do not know here, though your King will do his best to change that. Already we talk of it. Already I tell him about painters like . . . like Masaccio, and Lorenzo Monaco, and my own friend Masolino da Panicale who is even now painting frescoes in the Brancacci Chapel of Sta Maria del Carmine in Florence, while here you just fight and quarrel and hate one another across the Borders. You waste so much time, which could be spent in creating beauty, and peace and love. Especially love . . ."

He was looking at her, soulfully, so that she laughed again, realising he was a practised flatterer, then Archibald caught her arm, bowing stiffly to her admirer as he led her away.

"What do you mean by allowing that . . . that little posturing crab to admire thee?" he asked, angrily. "He is as soft as a woman."

"Do not be sure of that, Sir Archibald," Margaret told him, her eyes full of mirth, yet she felt oddly pleased by his jealousy. "A man with Faith such as his, will surely make his mark on the Church, though there's no denying that he also has secular interests . . ."

"But not with my wife," said Archibald, and she said no more.

The Lord of the Isles had not attended the Feast. The Earl looked for his arrival and was uneasy about the look in the King's eyes when his non-appearance was marked.

Sir Thomas had not agreed with his King on that other notorious occasion when the Chiefs of the Highlands and

Islands had been invited for just such a time of merry-making, and on obeying the summons from the King, had found themselves in prison instead. James had laid a trap for them. It was the only way he could catch wild animals, as he put it to the Earl.

"Lest I offer them food to eat from my hand, they come not at my bidding," he said. "Now I shall make an example of some of them, and let the rest go free to tell of my wrath. If they be not tamed, I shall find other ways."

The Earl had ventured to reason with the King.

"The Nobles need to trust thee, Sire," he said. "If you must spring a trap, then do it without treachery."

"Treachery!" thundered the King. "They are the traitors! They wad hae Kingdoms of their own and summon me to pay allegiance to *them*. In the time of my Uncle, the Duke of Albany, who ousted my father from the Throne and killed my brother when he grew to manhood and was fit to rule, the matter of allegiance was settled. Have thee no mind of Harlaw, Sir Thomas, when the Lord of the Isles gathered himself an Army and marched out of the mountains and fought the Lowlanders at Harlow near Aberdeen. Has not thine own son played the game called Red Harlow when he was a boy at school? Donald, Lord of the Isles, got his deserts that day, and now his son, Alexander, comes along to roast me. I let him go when I had him in prison, but I should have kept him there. He sent me a note of hand offering peace now that no man will fight with him against me. Peace! As though he were also a King. I have told him he maun come and ask pardon. I will *not* have the Nobles so proud that they set themselves up above their King."

He glowered and the Earl saw that he was looking at Sir Robert Graham who was talking with Sir Alexander Blair.

"We have laws now, Sir Thomas, where none existed before. I rule firmly, but I make my laws with the help of the Privy Council, which includes thyself, and with the help of Parliament which includes people of note in our country, down to the Wise Men appointed by our small Barons and burgesses to speak for them. Our country has been kept poor and without education while obstinate clans war with one another, and only join together to keep out the common enemy."

He stared at his old friend.

" I have thy support, Sir Thomas?"

" Aye, Majesty."

" Aye . . . and the support of thy son, Sir Archibald?"

Sir Thomas' eyes flickered, then steadied.

" Aye, Majesty."

"See to it, my Lord Earl. See to it."

* * *

It was not as rich and colourful as the English Court, thought Margaret, as she ate the food laid before her on silver plates, yet there was a robust dignity about it which was the more impressive. The gowns of the ladies were not extreme in fashion, and she saw her own gown being admired since the material was of finer weave.

The Noblemen were more colourfully dressed than their ladies, but their clothing went well with their great strength. Heavy locks of hair and beards had been trimmed and there was much gaiety and laughter, while the King played the lute, and recited poems he, himself, had written.

Some of the older Nobles looked as though they would have preferred to be riding to battle, but the younger ones listened with attention.

The following day Margaret wore more sober garments as she accompanied Archibald and the Earl, along with all the other Nobles and Courtiers to the Church service in Holyrood Church. Once again she had to get used to the simplicity of her surroundings, yet something in her responded greatly to the service. James was concerned for the poor in his Kingdom, and gave orders to the monasteries that the poor and the needy must be succoured before indulging themselves in rich trappings, as Archibald explained to Margaret, though she looked at him and wondered if she detected sarcasm in his voice.

" It is ever easy to sin freely, then ask God's forgiveness," he said.

"I have heard that other Kings do not listen to the voices of their own people when they ask for help."

"There are too many in the Kingdom holding out begging bowls," said Archibald. "They deserve to have their cheeks branded."

It was very cold in the Church, the thick stone walls keeping out the warmth of any sunlight, and the Bishop's melodious voice was like to send her to sleep. Suddenly all thoughts of fatigue left Margaret as there was a commotion at the door, and a man thrust his way forward, clad only in shirt and breeches, his sword in his hand.

Archibald leapt to his feet, reaching for his own sword, but the slender dark figure of Alexander, Lord of the Isles, was too quick for any of them, and he ran forward towards the King, who gazed at him sternly, making no move to defend himself.

There was a gasp throughout the Church, as the Nobles and their ladies rose and leaned forward, but already Alexander was on his knees, holding out his sword to the King, the point in his own hand. It was a traditional plea for forgiveness, and Margaret felt the relaxing of tension around her. So the King had won! The Lord of the Isles was, indeed, willing to make peace.

"Arrest this man!" thundered the King. "We will attend to him *after* we have attended to our Lord God!"

Margaret watched as the proud Alexander, his face dark with humiliation, was bundled out of the Church, and James ordered that the Service be continued.

She was again aware of Archibald's anger and tension as he stood at her side. Why could not the King have accepted the sword and forgiven the Lord of the Isles? she wondered. Yet was not that what everyone expected the King to do? Only James had his own ideas on governing his country. He never did what was expected of him, when put to the test in this way.

Nor would Archibald discuss any of this further, as they rode back home towards Balgennan, though with every mile Margaret felt glad to leave the Court behind, and to look forward to the peace and tranquility of the ancient Castle set above the rocks on the coast.

The Earl looked tired when they arrived home and Margaret saw Gavin running about in all directions, giving orders to the grooms to attend to the mounts, and having warm water and clean clothing ready for the Earl and Sir Archibald.

"Thy new maidservant will help attend thee," he told Margaret. "She arrived but a few hours ago. She is helping Sarah Cowan . . ."

"My new maidservant . . ."

She looked with bewilderment as a tall fair young woman came towards her boldly, her simple sober garments only emphasising her beauty. Margaret had no difficulty in recognising Lady Helen Stewart.

"That's well done," said Sir Thomas, hardly glancing at the girl. "I told thee to hire a new maidservant."

She bobbed a curtsey at him demurely, then turned and bobbed another at Sir Archibald, her eyes dropping though there was a smile on her lips, almost of secret amusement.

Margaret saw the colour leaving her husband's face and the marks of his illness again were well defined.

"Take my cloak to my bedchamber, girl," she commanded, and Nell Stewart looked taken aback, "and I shall require warm water to remove the stains of travel, and clean clothing. My maidservant from our journey is also travel-stained and weary. Sarah Cowan will help thee."

"Sarah Cowan is not here," put in Gavin.

"Not here!"

"She walked out yesterday, saying she wished to collect wild raspberries for a sweetmeat, and elder flowers for a herbal drink. She . . . she never returned."

Margaret felt a sense of panic rising in her again.

"Search the area . . . search the whole of Balgennan. Sarah *must* be found."

"I have already sent the men out to seek her," said Gavin, his face unnaturally white. "We will do our best to find her, Lady Margaret."

"Was she alone?"

"We know not."

" We must find her,' said Margaret, in some distress. Sarah was her last link with her old home.

" We'll find her."

Sir Archibald's hand was on her arm, and there was kindness in his voice. He had turned away from Nell Stewart, after the first start of shock, and Margaret was glad he had command of himself. Her worries over Sarah were enough, without having the problem of Archibald and Nell Stewart thrust on her so suddenly.

The Earl had gone to his quarters, and Margaret turned away with Nell.

" Will you wish me to lay out your clothes in the small chamber next to Sir Archibald's room?" asked Nell, slanting a glance at Margaret.

She felt the colour stain her cheeks, and glanced quickly at her husband.

" We occupy the chamber of the Heir of Balgennan," she said, haughtily, and swept ahead, leaving Archibald to follow. It was time the question of their marriage was resolved, thought Margaret, furiously.

Sir Archibald must make his choice.

NINE

The question of choice was made for Sir Archibald that
night after Margaret had had a private talk with Nell Stewart.

" What do you mean by leaving the shelter of the cot house?"
she asked, severely. " Do you not know that you could endanger
the lives of all of us? His Majesty puts his trust in the complete loyalty of the Earl, and should he find him sheltering a
member of the family he considers his enemy, he would like
to have the lot of us bedfellows with the Lord of the Isles."

" He is a tyrant. I hate him," said Nell, sullenly.

" I would not blame thee for such sentiments," Margaret
admitted, " but I cannot ally myself with thy people. My
grandfather, Sir Andrew Colville, lost his estates through
Albany. Were it not that my father was his Uncle's heir, we,
too, would be paupers. Tyranny is to be found on all counts,
Lady Helen."

" But thy family lives happily and in peace."

" And would succour thee, if we manage to achieve safe
conduct to Wrykin Hall. I intend to send a party of horsemen
to carry news and gifts to my parents' home. It could include
a young boy, if boy thee will be for two days ride."

" The witch suspects my presence . . . "

" The witch! "

" Janet Armstrong. She whom they call a witch. She witched
me from the hovel and spied upon me. The cottager grew
afraid, and I had to find my way to the Castle, and told Squire
Johnson that I was thy new serving maid. He remembered the
visit to the hovel."

" So Janet Armstrong knows, and would harm Balgennan if she could."

Lady Helen shrugged.

" I care not about Balgennan any longer. I hate the Earl. Now I hate Sir Archibald . . . "

" Silence! " said Margaret, her hand itching to slap the girl. She looked up to see Sir Archibald standing in the doorway of the chamber, his hooded eyes following the slender sprite of a girl with the golden hair.

" I would gladly give her to you," said Margaret wearily, " if it could be accomplished honourably." Fatigue goaded her to indiscretion when she saw the coquettish look the girl cast in her husband's direction. " I cannot even offer her as a concubine."

Archibald grew red with anger and turned on her furiously.

" Hold thy tongue, wife! I make excuse for you since I know your anxiety for Sarah Cowan, and your fatigue hangs over thy head, but the Lady Helen does not deserve insults."

" No. I ask pardon," said Margaret.

" What are your plans, because if you have none, I will make my own."

" That she should go to Wrykin Hall, in the party carrying my messages and gifts to my parents."

" Nell Stewart should be grateful."

Nell Stewart did not look very grateful, but Margaret could see the droop of tiredness in the girl's mouth.

" Go to your chamber," she said. " My husband will maid me. We can talk again on the morrow, but rest well. The journey is tiring."

Nell Stewart lingered, looking at Sir Archibald again. Margaret turned away. If there was love between them, she did not want to see it. Finally the girl left the chamber and made her way to the small bare room nearby, reserved for maid servant to the Mistress of the household.

" How do I maid thee? " asked Sir Archibald.

Margaret showed him the many hooks which fitted her dress and clumsily he undid them, then turned her round.

" For better or worse," he said, roughly.

" Aye, it was so, but I now grow weary enough not to care."

" My own troubles put the Devil in me," growled Sir Archibald, " but I have made my choice. We put the Lady Helen in safety and try to save the honour and safety of Balgennan."

" With all thy heart?"

" With as much as I can give. I have seen thee look at the Squire."

This time Margaret was put to the blush.

" He is a fine fellow. But I would fain have played with the moon as a child, and was given a wooden doll in its stead."

" Now you grasp a wooden-head . . . myself . . . to show Nell Stewart you are truly Mistress of the household."

" You are no wooden head."

" Nor a pretty fellow! "

She turned to look at him, her gown slipping to the floor, the hooks undone.

" Is it so?"

Suddenly he turned from her, his face hard and white.

" I grow weary of my duty . . . my duty to my King and the Country . . . my duty to my Earldom . . . my duty! I will come to thee when it need not be my duty, Lady Margaret, when nothing matters but ourselves."

She watched him go, knowing an inner rage and frustration second to none. Was their marriage to be some sort of sword-play . . . thrust and parry . . . thrust and parry? One thing she was sure. The Stewart girl must go . . . and soon!

The Earl was in fine humour over the Wolf Hunt, though it was like to postpone Margaret's plans for the removal of Nell Stewart. Few heads of wolves were claimed nowadays, and the Earl was convinced that they were being brought to a minimum by zealous hunters.

Squire Gavin had been riding round the Estate, accompanied by a few good men, and they found no evidence of deliberate breeding to claim rewards when other sources of income would be small.

Sir Archibald, too, was shouldering a goodly part of his father's burden in seeing that their lands were cultivated by tenant farmers, according to the Law, protecting their people from thieves and robbers who were like to roam the country-side, and to quash quarrels at their source, lest the heat of them ignited a flame like to roast more than the original participants.

The Earl's high humour was in seeing his household settling down into good order.

He had eyed Nell quizzically, as she frisked about, occasionally coquettish when she realised she could cause Margaret the more mischief in this way, and also make Sir Archibald the more uncomfortable.

His own feelings were in a sad state, torn between his old passion for Nell Stewart, and respect for his lawful wife. Besides which Lady Nell exasperated him more than enough by her wilful behaviour, like to bring herself to the notice of the Earl, instead of serving Margaret quietly until the arrangements could be made for her journey south.

Of Sarah Cowan there was no sign at all, and Margaret realised with a growing sense of horror that another person, close to her, had disappeared completely and was like to have been murdered. She had a word with Gavin about it.

" Make every enquiry," she urged. " Surely you must know that the woman was dear to me, having known me since a babe."

" Rest assured, Lady Margaret, I'm doing all I can," he told her. " Whilst seeking out the protectors of wolves, we also have sought out the hidden places where she might be lying, having fallen and injured herself, and enquired at cot houses lest she had wandered into one for shelter if her mind be a-wandering. The people are kindly to unfortunates like themselves unless they be under famine, when they forget that the priests have taught them to love one another."

" There are times when it is hard to love one another, or to love ourselves, Sir," said Margaret, her eyes on Nell, who was going to need her ears boxed if she did not show some sign of remembering that she was her maidservant and not Queen of the Realm.

Gavin watched the direction of her gaze. The new maid was unusual for such a task, and he wondered at the peasant mother who would bring up her daughter so foolishly as to give her such lily-white hands, unused to toil, and allow her to grow such an abundance of golden locks without braiding it sufficiently under a cap. The girl was like to ape her betters.

" I could take that child to my mother's household," he offered. " My mother would be like to mould where her own mother . . . or Mistress Geddie . . . has left us virgin clay. She requires training in the art of service. She should go into the Dairy, then she would be happy to work on her mistress's dresses."

Margaret bit her lip, then dropped her voice.

" I'm remembering thy vows to protect the House when you became Squire to the Earl. Did you make such a vow?"

" Aye, indeed," said Gavin.

" Then I had better tell thee, the maidservant is the Lady Helen Stewart, last of Duke Murdoch's household, who escaped the block when the King ordered that their blood be spilled. Sir Archibald has been hiding her. He was her admirer in happier times, but their fortunes forced them apart. Now we are all in danger while she remains under our roof, but I hope to get her away to Wrykin Hall, and my mother's protection, and good sense."

" God in Heaven! " gasped Gavin. " Why did you not tell me before? I would have made . . . other arrangements for the wench."

" She is a Lady born. I felt she had suffered greatly already. Sometimes one saves the drowning kitten, feeling that it deserves life having cheated death."

Squire Gavin seemed to be watching the girl with fresh eyes.

" She is a delicate lady. I was oafish that I did not heed that until now."

" Do not languish over her delicate breeding," said Margaret, rather tartly. " Only be aware of her true identity. The Earl must never know she has been close under his eye, or he would be like to march us all back to Court. He does not recognise my maidservant as the Lady Helen. Murdoch's friends were never his."

" What would you have me do?" asked Gavin.

" I will make plans, and ask your help in carrying them out,"
she told him. " They will need someone with a cool head.
Just keep your eye on her, Gavin, and I will gather my
messages together to send to Wrykin. If only Sarah had been
here . . . "

She forced back unaccustomed tears. She and Sarah Cowan
had not always been in agreement, and she had hectored the
old woman, but now she missed her beyond belief.

" I could do with another woman to accompany the girl on
the journey, or send her as a boy."

" Let me but consider the matter," Gavin told her. " We
need all our wisdom to keep her identity among ourselves."

*　　　*　　　*

Margaret found that she was kept busy arranging the household for the day of the Wolf Hunt. Large tables were set out
with great platters of meat and fish, and sweetmeats made
from honey, nuts and fruit. The shadow of Sarah Cowan
walked beside her, knowing that the old woman had been out
gathering fruits for a recipe of her own to show the other maid-
servants, when she disappeared.

Sir Archibald had ordered the men abroad repeatedly, to
search every inch of ground throughout the Earldom, but
there was no trace of her to be found. So Margaret concerned
herself with household affairs, and saw to it that there was
enough food for hungry men, scolding Nell Stewart into more
labours than her nature inclined.

Already the other servants were looking askance at Lady
Margaret's new serving woman who was inclined to languish
sulkily.

The day of the Hunt dawned with fair weather, but cold,
and Sir Archibald was in fine fettle with the good colour of
health once again in his cheeks. He towered over Squire Gavin
by several inches and sat his horse well.

The Earl sat in a corner of the Great Hall, ready to check
that all his farmers and their labourers had answered the call
to the Hunt, and to receive the fine of a sheep if they could

not, or would not, attend. Few sheep were received on that day, the day being one of pleasure, unlike the destruction of crows which had to be destroyed without the merriment of companionship, and which was a wearisome task, the creatures taking to wing at first rustle. Many a good wife saved her five shillings thriftily, and paid that sum as a fine to have trees chopped, where the crows were most prolific, so that they could no longer be used for nesting.

For Margaret the day of the Hunt was tiring, knowing that the curious eyes of their tenants looked at her boldly or shyly, assessing her as the new bride to the Heir. The Earldom was law-abiding, and well-run, so that the landlords and farmers lived in harmony. A few disobeyed the Laws and were punished, though the punishment was fair and quickly meted, without shilly-shally, and without relish. Seeing that the Lady showed zeal and energy, and was in full command of her household, Margaret could feel that she had gained approval and respect.

Soon there was much merry-making as a small pack had been raised, and whelps' heads were brought into the Great Hall, and placed before the Earl, who solemnly paid over two-pence as a reward. Margaret had to turn away at the sight of blood-stained hands and clothing, though she remained in command of herself.

She sat down for a moment near the inglenook of the great blazing fire of logs and coal, to warm the chill from her bones, and shortly a servant maid came up to her and bobbed a curtsey.

" There is a woman in the courtyard, near the kitchens, who would have a word with thee, my Lady," she said.

" What woman?"

The servant, little more than a child, looked frightened, and Margaret wondered at the choice of messenger. She had no stomach for beating the young serving maids.

" My Lady, it is the . . . the servant who once held sway over our kitchens . . . Janet Armstrong . . . "

" Janet Armstrong! "

Margaret's face began to grow scarlet with anger. She remembered the woman flaunting herself before her as though to challenge her will, and how she had made short shrift of her. Then she looked round for Nell Stewart, with a hint of fear in her heart, but saw that the girl was engaged in cutting up bread into tiny squares so that on this occasion, the landlords and tenants could be given a taste of this delicacy.

Had the woman come to denounce them, in the name of the King, for harbouring a member of a family declared traitor? Were they to be put to the horn and declared traitors themselves? Swiftly she got to her feet.

" Show me," she commanded the girl and followed her down through dark corridors of chilly stone, past the busy kitchens where the sheep were being roasted, and out through a low entrance to the side of the Keep where she rarely lingered, but for inspection. The woman was waiting for her, clad in plain homespun instead of the gaudy colours beyond her station, which she had worn in the Castle.

" What brings you to me, Woman?" Margaret demanded boldly, determined not to be intimidated.

" A guest, my Lady."

" A guest?"

Margaret's heart was beating loudly, though she managed to look calm, and faced the woman haughtily. So she had found out the identity of her serving woman, and knew she was Lady Stewart.

" How can a guest of mine concern thee?" she asked, coolly.

" No guest of thine, my Lady. The woman is *my* guest."

Margaret managed to smother her surprise in curiosity.

" Cease talking in riddles, Woman."

" Mistress Sarah Cowan, my Lady."

Margaret's knees felt weak as she stared at the woman, then she led her into the kitchen quarters, to a small room where Janet Armstrong at one time had spent most of her days.

" Explain yourself, Mistress Armstrong, and if any harm has come to Mistress Cowan through thy manifestations . . . "

" Harm! Haven't I nursed the woman to health when she was a-wandering in body and mind? Haven't I dosed her with herbs to kill her fevers and quiet her thoughts?"

" Then she is well?" asked Margaret, eagerly.

" Well in body, but . . . her terrors have robbed her of brightness."

" Why must you come now, and not when most of the armed men of the Castle were scouring the countryside for the woman? Why keep her hid?"

Janet Armstrong stared boldly.

" She is but a poor woman, one of my own kind. I thought she had run away from punishment, or been thrown to the winds. Such things happen from the Castle walls, my Lady."

Margaret flushed, knowing that she was being reminded of the woman's own removal from this household.

" Where is Sarah?"

" She is safe in my cottage, but she is full of her own fears. I can keep her the longer, but . . . " she shrugged, " . . . we eat but sparingly. Her stomach would be the better filled under the Castle roof. She grows weary of possets of nettles and dandelions, with a rabbit when he hits my snare."

" So you want merks?"

Again the woman shrugged and eyed her slantingly.

" It was said the serving woman is of value to you and worth a merk. But I succoured her because she is a poor woman and was sick, and ask no reward, but I show thee I bear no ill-will. I give thee my respect as a fair Mistress, and ask leave to return to this household as a serving maid, or scrubbing woman at the wash-tub."

" The Earl . . . "

The woman laughed harshly. " Think ye that I'm the first under his roof he has thrown from his bed? There are many among the labourers who have had a taste of comfort in return for favours easy to grant. Aye, and now bring up the young who will owe blood loyalty to the House. Think ye I care that I am one of many?"

" I do not trust thee," said Margaret, after deliberation. Part of her was joyful that Sarah Cowan was alive. But there was something repelling about the woman, and she coud not rid herself of a feeling of distrust.

" I would have to see Sarah," she said at length.

" I am ready to receive thee in my home," Janet Armstrong said, formally.

' The Squire shall accompany me," Margaret decided.

" On the morrow, when the household rests," the woman said. " The revelry will give sore heads to a few in thy service."

" Revelry?"

" The Wolf Hunt, my Lady. As darkness falls, torches will be lit in the courtyard and there will be dancing to the pipes and ale to lighten the feet. The poor labourer will forget the pain in his belt since it will be vanquished by the feastings, and the fat farmer's conscience will be eased by the sight of his men set in enjoyment of their lot. The wenches will forget that they could bear the burden of merry-making to the day of reckoning lying ahead, and the loons can claim that they remember nothing, and refuse responsibility with the ale fumes reeking in their heads. Oh aye, my Lady, there will be revelry. I advise thee to retire in grace, lest a numbskull mistake thee for a pretty one, in thy youth."

" Enough! " cried Margaret.

" I will bring the Squire to thy cottage on the morrow and pay thee the merks for attending my serving woman. For this, if she is well at thy hands, I owe thee my thanks."

" I would beg more than thanks," said Janet Armstrong. " I beg to serve once more within the Castle walls. The cottage can grow cold in winter and harsh for a poor woman."

" I . . . I'll think about thy request," said Margaret, wishful that it had not been made. " Take food from the table for Sarah . . . and yourself."

" My thanks, my Lady."

The woman walked boldly out of the room and swung along the corridor to collect her food, informing the servants that she had leave from Lady Margaret, even as she laughed with some, and hailed others she had known.

Margaret saw her stop before Nell Stewart, weighing the girl up appraisingly.

" Like the lady born," said Janet Armstrong, softly. " Such airs and graces for a serving wench! "

She left, hips swaying, the food in a bundle swung on to

her back. Her dress was old and darned, her hair long and rich, her body sinewy but healthy, and she lacked the slow shuffle of women servants.

Margaret enquired for the Squire and learned that both he and Sir Archibald were still out on the Hunt. Later the sounds of revelry built up and the Castle seemed to reverberate with the noise and shouts and screams of laughter, and occasional pain as excitement brought blows on younger heads for rowdy behaviour.

The Earl had grown expansive with wine and ale, and Margaret began to search for Nell Stewart, knowing that she must order the girl to her chamber, lest it be thought that she was, indeed, a mere serving wench and to be used as such.

She was in the throng, her eyes bright and bold, her body lithe as she danced a jig to the pipes. With a sense of horror, Margaret realised the girl had been drinking ale and was in the thick of the merry-making. She fought to grab her arm.

" Come with me, girl," she commanded, loudly, and Nell peered at her, then pulled her arm away.

" 'Tis the servants' night for having fun," she said, " and I am a maid servant to the Lady. I claim my rights."

" That is just! " a young fellow cried, jovially. " The maid claims her rights. She'll have plenty of rights ere dawn, I promise. She shall have her entitlement."

" Come here! " cried Margaret, rather wildly, grabbing the girl's petticoats as she whirled away. The torches had been lit, and the heat generated nauseating body odours from unwashed bodies and clothing, either through economy of cleansers, or time, or belief that to lose one's dirt was to lose one's protection against the elements.

Then she saw Squire Gavin, and rushed to grab hold of him amid taunting and merriment, though she no longer cared, gasping out her request that Nell Stewart be protected.

" Rest easy, my Lady," Gavin told her, though he, too, seemed merry with ale, but yet able to stand square on his legs and to have a head clear of fumes for taking hold of a situation and obeying orders. He'd had to remain clear-headed in the past, against treachery. It was times like these when an enemy could creep towards the Castle, and break through their defences to slip a dagger under the Earl's tunic, but he had never yet been caught sleeping when his master required protection.

Now the Lady Margaret was appealing to him to protect the Lady Stewart, who could not make up her mind whether to remain the Lady born, or join the common throng. He could see her fair hair, which had escaped from under her douce cap, flying about like the tail of his golden mare, Bess, as she danced and twirled to the heady music. He grabbed her, and hung the scarlet sash which marked him as the Squire, and Master of the Wolf Hunt, round her neck.

"I claim thee my partner," he shouted ringingly, and a few of the young bucks fell back, their disappointment momentary. There were other wenches, plumper and more ripe, though this one looked cool as a lily in her white serving gown. They durst not temper with a maid claimed by the Earl, Sir Archibald, or the Squire, and it was seldom the Squire claimed a wench.

"I would wish for another," said Nell Stewart, scornfully.

"He is on duty with his father, the Earl."

"I do not mean Sir Archibald. He is like thyself, old and dull though thy years be few. You are an old man, Sir Squire."

She threw back her head and laughed, and Gavin resisted the impulse to slap her face.

"Thee are a slut," he told her, roughly.

Her laughter stopped abruptly.

"Is that how you would use me? As a slut?"

"I would use you as your behaviour merits. The Lady Margaret is concerned for you. She sends me as your protector."

"The Lady Margaret!" Her lip curled. "What does she know about being thrown to the winds? Has she ever been rescued from the cesspit?"

Her laughter had gone, and Gavin had a sudden glimpse of the misery and despair behind the façade of vivacity, or hauteur, according to her mood.

"What would your own behaviour be, in her place?" he asked.

He had extricated her from the crowds, and they strolled towards the Castle curtain, his hand still on the scarlet sash which he had thrown round her neck, and which he was using as a halter.

" I wad throw me to the wolf-pack before they were rounded up and destroyed. Or I wad achieve the same end by giving me to the Magistrate. My blood is bad, therefore I cannot breed other rotten apples for my Liege Lord's barrel. See, Sir Squire, my finger is pricked. See ye this red blood? It grows black with poison before thine eyes. Is it not so?"

" Hush thy bitterness."

" It is easy to say so. Has thy head been in the noose, Sir Squire, then prised free? Know ye the terrors of the unknown? They say I will be judged one day on an awful day of Judgement, and that my sins, being many, will confine me to roast in the fires of Hell. Can they be hotter than the fires in my heart, or in my soul?"

He towered over her, and found himself pulling her into the protection of his arms, then the soft flesh of her arms went round his neck and they melted into the shadows.

" Comfort me, Sir Gavin," she sobbed, and guided him wantonly.

" I cannot," groaned Gavin. " Thee are Lady born. I would have . . . my manhood would be cut off. For the love of Heaven, my Lady . . . "

" Nell," she whispered. " Just thy Nell."

She was softer than any serving wench, and Gavin felt that the ale fumes had lifted him to a plane of existence as he lay with Nell Stewart, straining from her to drop his seed that their sin might not linger in her to come back to shame them both, but she grabbed him as in a vice.

" Thee are wanton!" he cried, and she laughed hysterically.

" Thee should know better. I gave thee my maiden-head."

" 'Fore God," he whispered. " 'Fore God ye have destroyed me. However pure thy body, thy heart is wanton."

" Only for Squire Gavin," she said, nuzzling into his neck. He held her as he would have held a captive bird, and her tenderness entered his soul.

"You are more woman than anyone I have known," he confessed.

"And I claim you as my man."

"No! It is madness. It is the night of dark blue velvet and the stars, and the revelry after a day spent on the chase, and ale in our stomachs with reeking fumes to dull our brains. It can't last."

She grew quiet.

"No. Nothing can last for Nell Stewart."

Gavin was remembering his vows of chivalry with renewed horror. He had broken all of them by taking Nell Stewart while she was under his protection, and his mind seemed to dart like sword thrusts, this way and that, to seek a solution to the situation in which he found himself. How had it happened? Could his world change for him in the space of five moments in time?

"My time is all but served," he said, after a long silence while she sat beside him like a small ghost in her white dress, the pale hair glowing in the faint light of the torches. "The King could dub me Sir Gavin next time I am called with the Earl. I would be given extra land, though it be barren land, but I know well how to nurture it, and it can be made sweet and fertile. My mother would welcome thee as my bride, and it would not be unseemly, as it might have been if thy family . . ."

"Had still been all-powerful and in its rightful place," she said, bitterly. "I have a minor Baron having to risk his future honour to wed with me."

He grew hot under his linen shirt.

"We cannot kick against change. And Nithrie is no mean hovel. I risk everything, my home, my lands, my people, by offering to wed thee, and to protect thee."

"Oh be at ease," she said, muttering impatiently. "There is no need to make a feast of it. I told you nothing lasts for Nell Stewart. Neither will thy seed last in me. I will not put thee to shame. Tomorrow our eyes meet without recognition. So be it."

His soul writhed with discomfort, and he thought about the

preacher and physician, Paul Crawar, who was still at Nithrie
with the warning in his ears that the Clergy were beginning
to seek out any who were lending an ear to his doctrines. He
had healed Gavin's younger sister of the choking disease by
placing a tube in her neck through which she could breathe,
and his mother, Dame Catherine Johnson, had been so grateful
that she insisted on giving hospitality to the man for as long
as he wished to remain in Galloway.

Crawar had immersed himself in the teachings of John
Wycliffe, who had been born almost a century before of a
Yorkshire family, whose local overlord was John o' Gaunt,
and it was through Wycliffe that a knowledge of religion in
their own tongue had first been brought to Englishmen.
Already many of the common people were demanding more
prayers and sermons, and less ceremonial in their Church,
and they were willing to listen to the fiery man who was Paul
Crawar, yet whose hands had the power of healing, even as
his words slipped into receptive ears and gave comfort and
solace to bewildered minds.

He had been in Bohemia, firmly supporting the Bohemian
Hussites, but recently a Lollard conspiracy in England had
been put down in great bloodshed, and Gavin knew that King
James was no sympathiser with the heretic, since he was
already doing much to further the cause of the Church. A
beautiful monastery was now being built at Perth, as Balgennan
knew to its cost, as well as that of the other Earldoms, since
a great deal of money was having to be raised to complete it.

As for Gavin, his thoughts of Nithrie were making him
turn pale. To be giving protection to Crawar, and now to have
Nell Stewart on his hands, was giving him no small disquiet.
He looked at her pale face in the dimmed lights and saw that
she looked almost ethereal, her delicate features luminous with
angelic beauty and purity. He could hardly believe she was the
same girl as the little fierce kitten who had clawed at him and
held him in a vice. Now she stared at him almost disdainfully,
yet with a silent appeal which confused and disturbed him.

" I ask nothing of thee," she said, proudly.

Gavin felt the blush of shame sweeping over his body. It

would be easy to creep away, to deny that anything had happened between them, yet if the King saw fit to dub him a Baron, he would ever see the black streak within himself which would show that he deserved none of it.

" No, we are bound together 'fore God," he told her, taking her hand. " Our destinies are linked, I know it full well. I cannot see an easy way ahead for the morrow or the day after, but I will ponder on it. If I but win my spurs, and ask thee to be my Lady of Nithrie, will you think about it? The Lady Margaret wishes you to go to Wrykin Hall in Cumberland, but thy chances of a good marriage in England would be no better than what I offer."

" Oh . . . offer! Offer! " cried Nell Stewart. " What care I for offerings? Can you not see that what I crave is neither riches nor possessions? Have you never felt the cold wind of being . . . alone? I wad only ask one thing of thee, and if I cannot have it . . . "

" What is it? " asked Gavin, uncomprehending. The girl talked in riddles.

" Oh, leave me alone," she said, rolling over to put her head on her arm. " I thought . . . I thought thee a chivalrous knight indeed. I have watched you and I see your glance on the Lady Margaret . . ."

" Hold your tongue," said Gavin, guiltily. " She is not for me, nor her husband for you," he added, brutally.

" Ah . . . Sir Archibald . . . he was a fair knight until he came by his wounds. I could have loved him. But for the fortunes of my family, we could have been wed, instead of having him joined to that imperious female. Ah yes . . ." she said, as Gavin reprimanded her angrily once more, ". . . I suppose I should not decry her, and had we been equals, I may even be liking her. She has done more for me than I wad do for her, as I grant you. Have done then, Sir Knight, and I go to serve my mistress with humility, and help her into her chaste bed. She rages inwardly because of it, but Sir Archibald's recovery will soon be complete and he will feel strength where it matters."

She laughed and Gavin drew back.

"Your tongue does not reflect your breeding," he said, shocked.

"Ah, but it does. I was brought up among men in my family. I'm no mealy-mouthed female. If you take me, then take an equal, Sir Gavin. Reflect on that to thy cost or . . . or happiness such as you might never have known. But I must have something in return."

"What?" he asked. "What could I have to give thee?"

"Thy love," she said, simply. "To an outcast, it is the most precious commodity. If I cannot have thy love, then keep thy distance, Sir Gavin. I want nothing else of thine."

She rose and slipped away from him into the shadows. Gavin sat for a time, then found a trough of water and put his head in it to cool him and chase the cobwebs before going back to his duties, and helping to throw out the tenants who were becoming quarrelsome and rowdy with the night's entertainment.

Sir Thomas sat, tired, at his place near the dying embers of the great fire, and gazed sourly at his Squire.

"Your absence was noted," he said. "I trust it was Squire's business."

Gavin's shame grew on him like a scarlet cloak, and the Earl growled, then gave a short bark of laughter.

"Aye, we cannot blame thee for thy manhood. Get me to my chamber, and throw out the hard heads. It has been a good day, Gavin, a good day. Now we make them pay for it by calling a wapinschaw. I lay ye a merk that the labourers have not practised a day with bow and arrow since the last wapinschaw, and will make fools of themselves and have their heads knocked. And on this very day . . . since it is past midnight . . . they will be digging their plot with iron limbs and sick stomachs."

Including himself, thought Gavin dolefully, as he carried out the last of his chores, knowing that only a few hours sleep lay ahead. The work of the Castle still went on even after a Wolf Hunt. They were often called upon to house a troop of soldiers or any of the Earls or Barons who might be travelling, and would need hospitality for the night. If Gavin had known who he would be obliged to succour, he would not have slept so easily that night, though indeed sleep was unwilling to come when bidden.

His head was full of the sweetness of a lily-white girl, Nell Stewart, who kept turning into a fiendish monster ready to cut the heart out of him.

TEN

Sir Archibald had watched the Squire leading Nell Stewart away from the mob, strolling with her into the dark shadows of the Castle Curtain, and he stared after them, his thoughts a torment. He felt deathly tired, and his fatigue was also a weariness of the spirit as well as body. In their chamber his young wife had already retired, her head aching with noise, and Sir Archibald felt inward shame and frustration that he was yet unable to go to her, and to court her into pleasure in their marriage. But ever the disquiet of his mind held sway over his body. He had believed that Duke Murdoch's family, and his supporters, had been unfairly treated. Now he was not at all sure.

Before his wounds, he had been a hothead, fighting side by side with his elders in France until his wounds sent him home. But during his days of agony, when his body sweats soaked his bed linen and his head swelled with fever, he had wrestled with the devils, and had cast out a number of them. Now he wondered if cruelty was justified in order to save the health and well-being of a greater number. He had sent an arrow through a rabid dog whose teeth would have bitten men to their eternal agony.

Yet in siding with those who would defy the King, he had made himself responsible for Nell Stewart, and might even have defied his father enough to take her to wife before he felt the great pain of a sword thrust, and the greater pain of a diseased wound. It was his wife who had begun to fight the nauseating poison of that wound, and who was, even now, trying to make Nell safe and unable to bring harm on their House, for his sake. She was capable and determined, but he wanted the softness of a woman's love and understanding. And always the shadow of her sister seemed to fall between them, and he could feel the seeking in her for the truth of Elizabeth's disappearance.

For a long time he had suspected the Armstrongs, his own enemies, but now he no longer had them watched by his henchmen for evidence of this. Too many had tumbled into the unknown, south of Balgennan on the Galloway coast. Innkeepers had been tried for the murder of travellers who had disappeared, and had been put to death, their bodies hanging from the gibbet as warning to others. When he grew well, his first task was going to be rallying his men for a new attempt to seek out the cause of these disappearances, and rid the countryside of this scourge, and he would have to be in full health again to pull his men together, so frightened were they of the unknown.

Sir Archibald found he was still looking for the return of the Squire, and Lady Nell, and he frowned darkly when they did not appear and the darkness began to fall, as some of the torches burned out and no more were lit. He turned away and went into his own quarters, seeing that his wife was still out of bed, but clad in a long flowing white robe, her beautiful dark hair falling about her shoulders, her face strong and beautiful with fine eyes and apricot skin.

Sir Archibald could feel the stirrings in his heart and wondered if now, he might not have regained enough strength in his loins to seal their marriage. He should have found a wench ere he shame himself before his Lady, but it might have been a worse shame to have to turn away from the wench, and hear her screeching laughter.

Margaret had turned to look at him and he could see the outline of her lovely body against the flickering of the firelight. Suddenly he wanted her, yet the fear of failure was still on him.

" It would have been prudent to guard your serving woman," he growled.

113

She flushed. " I ordered Squire Gavin to attend her."

" I have no doubt he is attending well," he said, " in the shadows of the Courtyard. I saw them go and their return long delayed for ordinary discourse."

" Perhaps his activities are such as would have pleased you," she threw at him, " but I trust his chivalry towards a Lady. He knows her identity."

" He . . ."

" I told him," she said, proudly. " He must know if he is to defend her honour. She has no interest in defending her own. The sooner I send her to learn better manners at the hands of my mother, the better."

" Aye," he agreed. " That is so."

She changed the subject abruptly.

" I want Squire Gavin to go with me to Janet Armstrong's cottage after breakfast," she said. " The woman claims she has Sarah Cowan in her keeping."

" Sarah Cowan! Why is she with Janet Armstrong?"

" The woman says she found Sarah a-wandering and gave her shelter lest she had been turned out of the Castle. She asks to serve once more in the kitchens as a reward for her services."

" That is a matter for my father."

" She claims he will no longer wish to use her favours, and that the others have not been penalised for freely giving comfort."

" She deserves to be whipped for impertinence," cried Archibald, stung by the frank discussion of his father's affairs.

" Tomorrow I will go early and see Sarah, and make sure if the woman's claims are true. I would have gone this evening but for the Wolf Hunt. I could not find you, and knew it would be unwise to go my lane."

" I am relieved at your good sense," said Archibald.

" I go early since I am impatient for the woman," she said. " What do I promise Janet Armstrong if her story be the truth?"

" You are Mistress of your household. Reward her with a few merks if that be more to your liking."

" I feel she is lonely away from the business of the Castle. She might work well, and she knows that I will not have her questioning my authority."

" I leave the matter in your hands," he said, then an unusual gesture, he took her small capable hands in his own. They were not the fluttering wings which were Nell Stewart's tiny hands, but stronger and more womanly. Gripping them in his own, he bent and kissed the palms.

" Goodnight, Lady Margaret."

" Archibald . . . Archibald, I am indeed thy wife . . ."

" And I have spent myself on the wolves," he said, though in a manner which made it difficult for her to believe him even though nerves and insecurity had turned his stomach to water. " I would be a dull bedfellow."

" You are a dull husband," she told him. " I return you . . . to the wolves! "

*   *   *

Gavin looked heavy-eyed next day as he rode beside Margaret to Janet Armstrong's cottage, a better building than the humble home which had housed Nell Stewart, since the door had been made of wood, and the chimney well set in a good fireplace, so that the walls were not darkened by smoke, and had been hung with drapes, no doubt filched from Balgennan.

Janet Armstrong wore clean clothing and had shoes on her feet which were normally bare except for the cold winter days. As Margaret stepped into the cottage she was minded of that other day, only a few weeks ago, when she went to find Nell Stewart. Now it was a cowering old woman who faced her from a seat in the corner.

" Sarah! " cried Margaret, running forward. " Oh Sarah! My heart has been cold with worry about you. Where have you been?"

Sarah shook her head, bewildered, and cowered back a little, then uttered a small cry as Gavin stepped forward, shielding her eyes with her arm.

"What ails her?" asked Margaret, sharply, turning to the other woman. "Why is she in such a fright?"

"She is better," the woman said, complacently. "Her body is better than it has been a wheen o' years. She has been given good dandelion root for her rheumatics, and chestnut leaves for her wheezes. See, she is plump with eating while I grow pale with the want of it, since I could not nurse the woman and yet hunt the hare, or snare a rabbit, or even catch a fish."

"Then what ails her?"

Janet Armstrong shrugged, her eyes wary.

"Ask her. Perhaps she will tell thee, my Lady."

Margaret knelt by Sarah's side, taking her gnarled fingers in her own.

"Sarah! Look, mistress, it's myself who has come for thee to take thee home to Balgennan."

Sarah shook her head.

"No!" she said clearly. "It is Devil's country. Home to Wrykin Hall."

Margaret looked at Gavin.

"We could send her to Wrykin with the next pack party," she said, in a low voice, "if it help her. She has been servant at Wrykin since childhood. I would want her with me, but if she is a-feared until her wits be dim, then she is better to spend her dotage at Wrykin. Can we seat her on my horse and she will ride with me?"

"Or I could carry her," Gavin offered.

"Let her get used to a man again," Janet Armstrong advised, as the old woman cringed away. "Whatever frightened her, it was nought in petticoats. I wad offer thee hospitality, my Lady . . ."

"I want no brew from your hands," said Margaret, then bit her lip. "How would I know it was not a drug to give you power over my soul?"

The woman laughed, a little bitterly.

"If I dared be witch, my bones would roast in Hell. My wine is refreshing as the woman could vouch, and if you will have none of it, then I ask leave to quaff a cup."

She drank some brightly gleaming amber liquid, her

eyes challenging Margaret, who looked askance at Gavin.

" I would crave a cup," she admitted, being thirsty from the dust, and after a moment he nodded.

Margaret accepted a draught of the wine and found it sweet and pleasant, with a flavour she recognised as elderflowers and hawthorns.

" So be it," she agreed. " I would like this woman to work in my kitchens, Squire," she told Gavin, " if there is no objection."

Gavin shrugged wearily.

" The kitchens are thy province, Lady Margaret."

" Very well, Mistress Armstrong. We leave now with Sarah Cowan. Your price will be paid."

" I thank thee, my lady," said Janet Armstrong, meekly.

She watched the strong young Squire lift the old woman on to Lady Margaret's horse, even as she struggled, her face distorted with fear.

" Come! " Margaret commanded impatiently. " This is enough. There is work to do without spending precious time on thy vapours. I am happy to see you well, Sarah Cowan, but we have wasted enough time."

She leapt lightly on to the horse, holding the old woman who had grown quiet now that Gavin no longer had hold of her.

Janet Armstrong looked after them, her eyes gleaming with a strange light, her smile triumphant. Margaret was too busy attending to Sarah Cowan to look back, and if she had, the smile would have told her nothing.

" You are quiet today, Gavin," said Margaret, her eyes twinkling. " Can it be that your head is as sick as your stomach?"

He did not rise to the bait. His thoughts were on Nell Stewart, and he could not forget that he held her slender body in his arms, and made her his wife before God.

" I ask pardon," said Gavin.

She sighed. " If the enemies of Balgennan wish to take our Castle, then they would be wise to choose the morning after a Wolf Hunt!"

He grew scarlet.

" I . . . I ask pardon. My mind was elsewhere."

" A female, I don't doubt. Have you found a light-skirt?"

His face showed the sweat of embarrassment, and she laughed gaily, wondering which maid had offered him comfort. She had no thought of Nell Stewart. That was to come later.

ELEVEN

The old woman was slow to recover, sitting about in the corner of a small room which Margaret kept for her own. After their initial distrust of one another, Sir Archibald and Sarah had come to have respect, each for the other, so that he was put out by her obvious reluctance to talk with him, and her cringing attitude when anyone went close to her, with the exception of Margaret.

"I thought to send her to Wrykin Hall with Lady Nell," Margaret told Archibald. "They would be protection for one another. I am going to seek permission from the Earl for a small party of horsemen to carry a few gifts to my mother, and to return with the remainder of my clothes. I would fain wear gowns which were favourites, though I had to leave them behind and travel light."

"I can well afford to put gowns on my wife's back," said Sir Archibald, proudly.

"Then guard your siller lest it part with thee too easily," Margaret told him, equably. "My gowns give me pride since the weave is different, and a woman enjoys gowns of distinction. Queen Johanna admired my gowns in Edinburgh. They were like to her own."

"So it is queening it now," said Sir Archibald, though there was laughter in his eyes. He was beginning to enjoy spirited conversations with his wife, and to miss her when she was out of the Castle. He had found himself watching for her return from the round tower, and not at ease till she was within the yett. He had been shocked to see the condition of the old woman and thought that a journey to Wrykin Hall would be the end of her.

"What ails thee, old woman?" he would ask Sarah, then offer her a honeycake as a token of sympathy.

Margaret found herself touched by his attitude, which was kinder than Gavin's, who seemed to have no thought for anyone save himself, since the Wolf Hunt. Margaret noticed that Nell Stewart had grown quiet and moody, and stared with lack of sympathy at Sarah Cowan. If she had her way, she would throw the old woman from the battlements as if she had been a dog in mortal sickness.

But gradually Sarah was beginning to recover, and on a quiet day, she suddenly rose and came to sit close beside Margaret. She had caught sight of Janet Armstrong, now employed at the Castle.

"She means thee harm, Mistress Margaret," Sarah whispered, and her young mistress was so pleased to have words of sense from her that she neglected to ask questions.

"Sarah! You are better. I can see . . ."

"She means thee harm," Sarah repeated dully.

"Who?" asked Margaret.

"It was a child," the old woman said, almost in a whisper, "yet narry a child. It was like an . . . an animal with hair grown wild and matted and a face as dark as sin. Yet it was like a child. And there was another . . . some other creature. I could hear its breath rasping, and they were coming at me with claws like an eagle. Then I heard the horsemen, and I cried to them, and the creatures slid back into the earth. But the horsemen passed by, and I ran and ran with briars catching my pettitcoats, and I fell down and lay on the good dark earth until the woman came."

"You owe her your life," said Margaret, simply.

The old woman had spoken in a sing-song voice almost as though she were reciting her dreams, and now she looked at Margaret.

"She has hatred in her heart for the Lady Margaret," she said, "who turned her out beyond the yett. Do not believe the honey and meekness of her tongue. Her herbs can heal, and they can drive men and women mad, and give them the sickness day by day so that she cannot be blamed. She has fear of burning as is her due, witch that she is."

Margaret swallowed, and tried to push the old woman's thoughts aside.

"You're so much better, Sarah," she cried.

The old woman leaned back tiredly, but nodded agreement, then the life went out of her and she fell forward off the stool which she had placed beside Margaret's chair. Margaret got up fearfully, then gave a great cry when she saw that Sarah Cowan was dead.

Lady Margaret's heart was shaken, and she called for Sir Archibald, who came running to help, and to comfort his wife.

"She was old and frail, and she had been through much sadness," he said.

"She had grown excited, warning me against Janet Armstrong," said Margaret. "Oh, Archibald, I fear again for the unknown thing which upset her. I'm sure Janet Armstrong is in league with this evil thing which surrounds us."

"Sarah was old," Sir Archibald said soothingly. "Why have fears within the Castle walls? The priest will say prayers over her grave and give her Grace."

"I should not have brought her on that long journey from Wrykin Hall," said Margaret. "And now we will have no woman to send with Nell Stewart back there."

"Forget about Nell," said Archibald, taking her close to comfort her. "Weep your tears and dissolve your sorrow. She was an old woman."

"And the last link with Wrykin," said Margaret, and wept out the last of her homesickness.

*　　　*　　　*

The days began to be weary ones for Lady Margaret who felt no inclination to make plans for the removal of Lady Helen out of her household, and often she felt that her low spirits were reflected in the rest of her household.

News came from Wrykin that there was unrest again on the

Borders, and that a band of armed men from Wrykin Hall, lead by Margaret's father, Sir John Colville, and her brother James, had been called upon by Cardinal Kemp to protect his Yorkshire property against the foresters of Knaresborough. Lady Mary was in charge at the Hall in their absence, and was not happy with her position, though she advised against any party of men being sent to exchange goods as Margaret had planned.

"I had better tell Gavin that any communication with my family must be postponed," said Margaret. "My maid must yet remain here."

"I grow weary of the problem," Archibald told her, and she found herself angry.

"The problem was your own making."

"Aye, but I yet grow weary, and so does the maid."

"She can learn patience. She can stay here for the present and we will not worry ourselves unduly."

Nevertheless Margaret was again experiencing the curious sense of inner chill which she was beginning to associate with ill news. It was a sense of foreboding, as though a cloud of evil was descending on the Castle. It gave her a feeling of sick dread, and she looked this way and that for its causes, though there was none.

The King and his lady, Queen Johanna, were at Crichton Castle in East Lothian, with their daughters and small son, James, where Sir William Crichton was seeking to entertain His Majesty after a tiring meeting of the Privy Council.

The Earl, accompanied by Squire Gavin, had been invited to join them and to indulge in some of the sports the King so loved to play, though Queen Johanna found Crichton Castle little to her liking.

"Sir William, your Chancellor, prefers to sit on his purse than build his Castle for civilised living," she complained. "The Keep is as ancient as his ancestors' bones, and his kitchens as like to the dungeon underneath. The Prince is like to catch fevers of its reek."

"Give him to Balgennan's Squire to guard, with his nurse, in the fresh sunshine, my dove," he advised. "The lad is earning his spurs and I will dub him Knight and grant him lands to swell his Barony when I am sure he is as faithful to me as his master, Balgennan. I move hither to his Earldom after Sir William and I complete our business."

She nodded, and leaned for a moment against his great chest. Queen Johanna envied no woman since she, alone, was wife to King James. She alone knew the courageous thinking and the stout heart of the King, and the torment which went with harsh decisions and mistakes.

" We will travel to Midlothian first," said the King, " and visit Borthwick, if thy woman's nature would fain see how siller maun be spent on fashionable improvements. It is some five years since I granted the good Sir William Borthwick a licence to crenellate at Lochorquhart, which was but an earthen mound of a Norman Castle. We hear he has been proudly boasting of a kitchen with fireplace big enough to roast an ox, with three windows to keep it sweet, and drains to carry away the stenches, and a garderobe with vessels to be emptied away from the well, so that the water may be sweet. He has built a Chapel within the Castle so that you may indulge thy worship and piety in comfort."

" I will be impatient to make the journey," said Johanna, her eyes sparkling. " At times I scarce remember what gentle living is like."

Laughing, he turned her round and slapped her bottom. Their palace at Linlithgow was full enough of gentle living for any woman!

" So my Queen has regrets! "

" Sore regrets," she agreed, rubbing her posterior. " Regrets that I married a bear, and not a man. How long do we stay with the good Chancellor here at Crichton?"

" A sennight. You maun tell his lady about Borthwick, for I think Sir William has a fondness for his old tower-house, though a new tower would not come amiss, as well as a new kitchen, I grant thee. He shall hear that opinion from me. He maun be short of bedrooms for housing a party, but he is your stout friend, my dove, should ever trouble come to thee."

"What trouble could come to me that cannot be dealt
with by my Lord?" Johanna asked lightly, then looked round
in alarm when James did not answer. The colour left her
face when she saw that his usual ruddy countenance was
pale and grave.

"I know not, sometimes my heart fails me. I rode out into
the Highlands once, into lands of grandeur yet which were
ever menacing, so that I knew I must deal firmly with their
Lords. But an old woman came out of her hovel and knelt
before me and told me to beware of the Firth of Forth. If I
cross it again, I may never return."

"She put a spell on thee. She should be marked as a
witch," cried Johanna with fear and anger. "She seeks to
frighten thee into dropping thy guard."

James shook his head, slowly.

"No, there was trouble in her eyes for me. I saw her look
anxiously upon me, and I knew her to be a loyal subject. I
know when my people are loyal, and when they only pretend
loyalty."

"Then do not cross the Firth," she cried.

Suddenly he was laughing again.

"Fear not, my dove. I just grow melancholy. It is the
fatigue of ever hearing complaints from the people, and trying
to hold the country as one. The Border raids are a drain on
our country, and the Marshals to keep the peace could be
better employed. Our soil could grow rich if the people carried
out my laws and cared for his patch to a man. There is skill
in the making of woollen cloth and our priests could educate
our people out of ignorance if they, too, obeyed my law. I
have sworn to make the key keep the Castle, and the brack-
bush, the cow, and I mean to carry out my laws, and when
educated men such as the Clergy are loth to work by my side,
then I maun fight twice as hard. The monasteries are rich,
but will not help the poor. They do not do their duty in works
of charity, and the common people are losing respect for the
monks. I see it happen again and again in the petitions of the
people who come before me.

"I have warned the Clergy that they see no further

than the tip of their long noses, and the people will not be
so treated all their days, and the days of their children.
Already I have protected them by seeking out heretics, though
only one has penetrated our land. Yet now and again I hear
whispers of another whom I maun bring to justice and cause
to be burned according to Law, yet no one need listen if the
monasteries obeyed my will."

" Do the fears for your person arise from the Church?"
she asked. " Is there treachery from beyond the walls of the
monastery?"

She looked at him with large frightened eyes, and he
laughed and hugged her again, so that her bones ached, but
with pleasure.

" Our good Chancellor's kitchens have filled my stomach
with food like to depress my spirits. I will go to the tennis
court, if it be good enough to be called a tennis court. There
is a better one at Blackfriars whence we go after Christmas."

Johanna responded to his mood, and called her maids to
dress her, even as the King prepared himself for a strenuous
hour.

" Tonight we make merry," he promised her. " I have com-
posed a new poem to thine eyes, and we will have music
and singing and dancing. If my vapours be not gone by
then, I give you leave to put my head in the noose, or to
stab me through the heart with my sword instead of thine
eyes."

A chill swept through her so that she shivered.

" Do not say so, James," she cried, " even in jest. It turns
my stomach to ice."

She went to seek her friend, Lady Catherine Douglas, who
could always cheer her up, passing the Chamberlain, Sir
Robert Stewart. He bowed low, and she acknowledged his
obeisance graciously. Yet the chill remained in her heart. Was
she developing James' intuition for whom to trust, and whom
to distrust? Yet he seemed to trust Sir Robert.

Queen Johanna's mood did not lift until she and Catherine
laughed indulgently when the young Squire, Gavin Johnson,
began to play football with five-year-old Jamie.

" 'Fore God, we break the law, Sire," said Gavin, and managed to save the ball before it bounced beyond the Curtain.

*   *   *

" What ails thee, lad?" asked the Earl, testily, as they rode for Balgennan once more. " Thy tongue is ever a-wagging, but now I fear that it has been cut from thy head."

" Perhaps the head which holds it gains sense and keeps it still," said Gavin.

" Very true if your looks were not as sullen as a tinker's."

They were approaching the Royal Burgh of Ayr, past cattle and sheep which were grazing on common ground, and entering the gates where the gatekeeper hurried to acknowledge the Earl and pass his party. He wanted to buy a gift for Margaret, which would please her, especially since he was bringing news that she would soon be hostess to the King at Balgennan, and he felt that the news might be received with as much nervous vapours as joy.

" What think ye?" he asked Gavin, as they rode down the Hiegait, calling out a greeting here and there to a burgess and his lady. " What might the Lady Margaret admire? A new bonnet? Gloves? Come on now, lad, I do not intend to linger at every booth, and I see some ragamuffins are letting their pigs run loose without ropes to lead them. 'Tis time His Majesty paid a visit to his town, and we'll spread the word, lad, so that they maun clean up the dung heap."

His nose wrinkled, and Gavin nodded as he followed the Earl through the throng, who fell aside to allow their progress. They passed under the banner of a candle-maker, where the Earl ordered fresh supplies, then he turned, again, towards the bonnet-maker's.

" Well . . . what think ye?"

" I know not."

" God's truth, man, but have you aged into your dotage? You are a youngling as is the Lady Margaret. Can a youngling not tell what pleases another?"

" I wad be like the Master of Misrule in a bonnet, Sir Thomas," said Gavin, and the Earl was like to aim a blow at his head, then his eyes crinkled and he laughed.

" Polish up your manners and keep your nose clean, and the King might dub thee if his stay at Balgennan be to his liking. But if your face keeps tripping your feet, I will not be sorry to lose thee, and find myself another."

The Earl aimed a playful box at his ears, and went to buy ginger, figs, almonds and wine.

" Lady Margaret was complaining about lack of pepper," said Gavin, helpfully, " and I wad care for a fine rice pudding once more, with raisins.'

" So it's your stomach that ails thee for its emptiness. Yet the King's table was well loaded."

" Aye,' said Gavin.

He could not confide to his master that he had lost his appetite with the looks His Majesty kept throwing in his direction. Truly, he had given him charge of the protection of his small son, who might one day be his own Liege Lord, James II, since the King was older than himself, but it had been the King's boast that he could sense true loyalty, and when one of his Barons was hiding things from him, and Gavin's heart had turned to water, remembering Lady Helen Stewart.

At first he had fond hopes of being dubbed Sir Gavin at Crichton, but the time had passed and instead he got glowering looks. How could he ever carry out his plans and take Nell Stewart from Balgennan, if he had no Barony where he could shelter her?

He could hardly wait to see Lady Helen again, even as he dreaded the meeting at the same time. Her soft body was a memory which drove him to distraction, yet she had a disdainful air when she sometimes looked at him as though he meant nought to her. He had been attracted by the Lady Margaret, but it was nothing to the thraldom in which he was held by Nell.

And the King was coming to stay at Balgennan! Gavin suddenly realised what this might mean, and almost fell to the ground as he realised how slow he was to realise the import of the visit. Would he be likely to recognise Nell Stewart? Could they hide the girl while the King was within the Castle walls?

Gavin swallowed and tried to take an interest in all the Earl's aiffairs. It was rare that they came to town, as the Earl was inclined to have the merchants attend him at the Castle.

After purchasing the gloves with the craftsman and his apprentice assuring Sir Thomas that they had been made of the finest leather, and reminding Sir Thomas that it had been traded with France under the Law of a Royal Burgh, and therefore finer than any he would find in a less privileged town, the Earl grew weary of the market and the depressing sight of the unfreemen on the opposite side of the street, proud that they were neither slaves nor beggars, yet chained to poverty by their social class.

Sir Thomas sought out a few merks and ordered Gavin to pass them on as gifts to be spent on filling their bellies ere they started to clean up the mess left by the market and the animals which ran about freely.

On the way to Balgennan, Sir Thomas reined in at the headland, and looked at the walls of his Castle which descended in a sheer drop to the lashing sea beneath. It was well protected, a fine Castle, but almost as old-fashioned as Crichton.

"We could do with improving the garderobe," he mused. "The Lady Margaret complained that it was fine and new in the days of our good King Alexander third, but hardly fitted for modern times. We maun arrange for a sweet-smelling contraption so that the dung is washed by the sea. I will see a craftsman about it. His Majesty must be made to feel at home."

"Aye, my Lord."

"And there is work for you to do, lad, making siccar of our defences."

"I will make sure of it," he promised, and went to chase the lazy servant to come and water the horses, and prepare the stores for the fresh supplies which would follow them from Ayr.

Inside his doublet he had concealed a pretty hair ornament. It was for Nell Stewart, and suddenly he looked forward to setting eyes on her fair beauty.

It was good, after all, to be home.

TWELVE

Lady Margaret had not been idle in the absence of the Earl. Sir Archibald had been left in charge of the Earldom, and the task had taxed his strength for a day, then another, but for the third he began to feel strength which had been lacking in his limbs since he was wounded. He began to breathe the freshness of the air as he rode round the Earldom, inspecting the land and listening to problems and complaints which were, at first, more numerous than his father had to deal with, but when the landlords and tenants saw that Sir Archibald had regained his manhood, then the complaints became fewer, and any made had to be genuine on pain of punishment.

Margaret was having her own troubles, after an encounter with Janet Armstrong, who had started her new bout of servitude with excellent service and manners of no fault.

Yet she found fault with the serving maid, Nell Stewart, and Margaret found her bullying the maid when Nell went to fill a pitcher of water from the well.

"Enough," Margaret said, surprised to see Lady Nell taking her scolding with due meekness, instead of the bold glances and disdainful manners she usually employed with the other servants.

"The wench is whey-faced, and no wonder," began Janet Armstrong. "She deserves a stick across her back."

"She is my concern, and none of thine," said Margaret. "She is no ordinary serving maid," hustling Lady Nell away, then she grew afraid of the maid's true identity being gossiped over by the servants, as she saw a look of triumph on Janet

Armstrong's face. Visiting packmen were ever ready with tit-bits of news to pass on, and sold their wares the more readily if they had fine pieces of gossip and scandal to go with them.

" She would make herself my concern, if she could," cried Janet, " and wishful for a potion to rid her of her shame. She should not lie so freely with a rogue who does not mean marriage. Mayhap she will need me . . . if she is no ordinary serving maid, my Lady."

Margaret was pushing Lady Nell up the spiral staircase to her rooms above before the words began to have meaning for her. The girl was beginning to look pale and ill, but she had thought it to be fear at the vulnerability of her situation, and the long delay in passing her to safety at Wrykin Hall. Now she turned her round and stared at her face and body.

" Are thee with child?" she asked, bluntly.

Nell returned the look sulkily.

" I know not."

Margaret resisted the impulse to box her ears.

" Have thee cause to be anxious for thy state?"

Nell Stewart's eyes suddenly blazed.

" If you must know . . . aye, my Lady."

" If a servant has forced thee . . ."

" I would not lie with a servant! "

She had tossed her head proudly and suddenly Margaret's heart began to grow cold with shock, and her mouth felt dry. It was all too easy to guess whose child Nell Stewart carried. Sir Archibald had spurned his wife, and it was easy to understand the reason, now that his woman stood before her. Margaret remembered that he had loved Nell even before he had agreed to take a wife. Rage and jealousy almost blinded her, and she had to turn away to keep herself from striking the girl's pale, lily-white face.

" Leave me," Margaret said, harshly. " If thee be slut, then take your punishment. If it were not for endangering Balgennan, I should have put thee outside the Castle walls."

For once there was no defiance in the girl, and Margaret could see that she was too full of fear to be pert.

That evening Archibald arrived home with the richness of good health in his cheeks, the dullness of fatigue gone from his eyes. Margaret had no idea that he could look so fine and handsome, but her heart was like a stone in her breast, so that she remained cool as a lily when he came to find her, and would have greeted her as husband to wife.

"My strength returns," he told her. "All day I have ridden and inspected the land, and dealt with the lazy and praised the diligent. My Margaret, the life flows rich within me again."

"And within thy paramour, Nell Stewart," she said, harshly.

"How so? Was she ever ailing?"

"She is ailing now," Margaret said, her eyes flashing, "and droops because she has been wanton and is with child, as thee well knows. You have spurned my body, and taken Lady Helen, and now the reaped rewards will be bitter. Will you petition the Pope for two wives, or for our marriage to be annulled?"

"I know nothing of Nell Stewart's trouble, nor can I believe she would be wanton."

"She denies nothing."

"She blames me? And you believe her?"

Archibald's face grew white and cold with disdain, and for a moment Margaret's heart failed her. Could she be wrong? Yet she had a feeling that the girl had not lied.

"I would ponder on it if you had taken me to wife, but now I care not to be your wife. I am glad you have spurned me."

"I was weak and lacked strength from my illness. If Nell Stewart blames me, she lies. I am accused unjustly, and feel anger enough to whip thee, and Nell."

He stalked out of her chamber, and she felt the womanish weakness of tears spill on to her cheeks. To be spurned for a girl like Nell Stewart! And now Nell carried a child, while she . . . Margaret's tears fell faster. She would give much to change places with Nell and feel a child within her.

The Earl's news was enough to put the last nail in Mar-

garet's coffin. The King was coming to Balgennan inside a
sennight!

She put all thoughts of Nell Stewart aside, in a frenzy of
preparation for the pleasure and comfort of His Majesty, and
the courtiers and soldiers he would bring with him, putting
rich hangings to the sunshine and fresh air to sweeten their
smell, and checking that the King would have finest linen
to rest him in his bed. The new extra stores were more wel-
comed and appreciated than the gifts of fine gloves and a
bonnet.

Lady Margaret showed that she was chatelaine of Balgennan, as servants rushed to her bidding, and even Nell was
put to tasks enough to keep her out of mischief. The Earl
watched with laughter peeping from his eyes, and slapped his
son on the back.

" Were she man and not woman, she would head her troops
with valour," he said. " You are lucky in your wife, my son."

Sir Archibald sought refuge in work of the estate, riding
round the tenants to prepare themselves for a wapinschaw,
and to dig their plot lest King James see neglect where none
might be, if the labourer rested long with his chin on his
spade.

Gavin had sought the first opportunity he could to have a
private talk with Nell, and found it easier than he anticipated,
so busy were his Mistress and the servants.

The kitchens were full of sweet-smelling spices as sweetmeats were baked, and hams roasted. Nell had helped to clean
cobwebs from the bedchamber, but her sickness had made her
faint for lack of air, and she slipped out to crouch down in a
corner of the battlements and there Gavin found her, his gift
of a pretty hair ornament held sheepishly in his hand.

" I brought you this . . . a pretty bawble," he told her,
awkwardly. " My thoughts were full of you, even as I guarded
the King's son, and played ball with him."

" You are a fortunate fellow," said Nell, sour-tempered
with nausea, " to guard the son of the King. My task is to
guard thy son, though he makes a torture of my body. Your
bawble will not help to rid me of my shame."

Gavin's face drained of blood, then it rushed back to his head, forming beads of sweat on his forehead.

" Are thee with child, to me?" he demanded.

" Who else? Think ye that I offer my favours to the henchmen? Yet my brains are addled enough. Madness must have come upon me, and still lives in my head. Already the Lady Margaret knows, but she does not know who has sired the child. She has no time to dwell on it for making the dust fly."

" We maun remove thee to a place of safety gan His Majesty set eyes on thee. He remains faithful to Queen Johanna, but his eyes rest on pretty women. He will have eyes for your lily-white beauty and your looks are so like unto Lennox, thy maternal grandfather, that he will soon be at bottom of thy presence here."

" Have no fear. Thy hands are clean, but for me, and you can deny me full well."

" My hands are not clean," he said. " The heretic, Paul Crawar, has had shelter in my household, and is now abroad, preaching his Lollard message in southern parts. If he is brought before His Majesty, and it is known that he rested at Nithrie, then the sword which might dub me Knight might be employed to remove my head. If I can but keep my nose clean until the King has come and gone, and I have gained my spurs, then I can take you to Nithrie as the Lady Helen Johnson. We could live a sweet life. You could be maidservant whom I have married for love, and no lie be told since I have great love for thee in my heart."

Suddenly the tears were drenching Nell's cheeks, and Gavin gathered her in his arms.

" My own heart is too heavy with fear," said Nell. " The servants know me for well-born, and not maidservant. Janet Armstrong has a black mind and a black heart. She will betray me, but only if she is sure that the Lady Margaret will suffer most through me."

" She shall be sent about her business," said Gavin, angrily.

" She is a witch, and holds sway over the common people and the servants of the Castle,' said Nell. " I have great fear of her. Some day she will do us great harm."

"Hush. It is only your sickness which dulls your mind."

He left her, hoping to have offered comfort, though there was none in his heart.

*　　　*　　　*

The King's visit was postponed. A King's messenger had come riding into the Courtyard, his horse heaving, to deliver a message to the Earl, who frowned, disappointed. He knew that Balgennan was no match for Linlithgow, but he was pleased by the way it had become an orderly household under Lady Margaret's control, though the girl had given herself tired looks and a wan face with all her pains.

Archibald, too, looked tired and in a sullen mood. It gave the boy a formidable look, though in truth, the Earl was proud that his son was not a man to be trifled with, and was no honey pudding when he was in his right mind and strength.

But now he perused the scrawled message from James, which said that he was delayed by affairs of State. The physician, Paul Crawar, had been denounced by members of the Clergy, having been caught preaching heresy to the common people. He had been turned away from one of the monasteries and, in hunger, had stood among the beggars outside a Church door, and been given a coat which he had later exchanged for meat at the door of a cot-house.

There he had given a lotion to an old man to heal a carbuncle on his toe, and the people had gathered to hear him preach against the doctrines of Rome.

News that he was waxing powerful came to the ears of the Bishops, and they had petitioned the King to try Crawar for heresy. The Earl was now summoned to sit on the Council which would give judgement on the man, and the Earl did not care for the task.

Sir Archibald refused to accompany his father.

"It would be small thanks for what the physician, Crawar, did to put my body into sweet health," he said. "I wad hae thought you more grateful to the man."

135

"I have shown my gratitude," the Earl stated, "but I deplore the man's ideas which make nonsense of his talents. He gives with one hand and takes with the other."

"I see nothing that he takes," Archibald protested. "I only see what he gives."

"He takes the spirits of men and bends them to his will. He takes from them the glory to himself, reflected in their eyes. His self-esteem is what he gains from the ignorant people who listen with hanging mouths to his words which seem to be rich in wisdom to their poor minds. Your years might bring you to manhood, but your brains do not."

"I'm sorry I disappoint you," said Archibald, "but I will not go and watch the man, Crawar, be condemned to burning. The King has not commanded me. I beg leave to guard Balgennan in your absence. My Lord Douglas, in Galloway, grows restless again and is raiding into Cumberland. It is rumoured that he grows impatient with Balgennan that we do not fight by his side, and looks askance at my wife, saying that she owes her allegiance to the English Crown."

The Earl flushed. He and the Earl of Douglas, his most powerful neighbour, were not always on the best of terms.

"Very well, I give you leave to guard Balgennan with thy life, and to defend the honour of the Lady Margaret."

*　　　*　　　*

Lady Margaret heard the news of the postponed visit with heartfelt relief, though she felt weary that her preparations would have to be made all over again. The King would find Threave more to his liking no doubt, though he sometimes showed wariness in the power of the Earl of Douglas.

Margaret had come upon Nell and Gavin Johnson whispering together in a long stone corridor near the Great Hall, and she turned on the girl.

"Have you no sense that you should imperil Squire Gavin and make him forfeit the honour which will soon be conferred upon him? Do you not know that he has sworn to be chivalrous at all times and must therefore listen to you, but be shamed by listening to a maid who offers her favours before wedlock?"

Lady Nell flushed, and turned to face Margaret defiantly.

"Perhaps I have more reason than most for speaking in private to Squire Gavin. We share the shame which grows within me by the day."

Margaret's eyes went to Gavin, her shock reflected in his, though he made no attempt to deny the charge, but nodded in acceptance.

"She speaks truly. The guilt is mine. I would have her to wife, and place her in safe-keeping at Nithrie, could I but arrange things that way."

"What things, besides this foolishness?" asked Margaret, her mind trying to adjust to this news. She had blamed Archibald falsely when, in truth, it was Gavin Johnson who was responsible. She had been very blind.

"The heretic was sheltered at Nithrie for some time before he left and ran his head into sore trouble with his trumpeting tongue. Now if I have not my hide skinned for Crawar, I will be in sore trouble for despoiling Lady Helen without the leave of God. The Earl prepares to leave for a meeting of the Privy Council with my Lord Douglas as one of the chief witnesses against Crawar. I will have to accompany him, and have but two days to settle Lady Helen."

Margaret's eyes were beginning to shine. Here was a solution worthy of all consideration and help. It would settle Nell Stewart in a good home, perhaps less than her station would have allowed, but better than the fugitive life she had been living. It would get her away from Archibald and his responsibility towards her, and it would remove her from Balgennan before the King made his visit.

"I could arrange it," she said, her eyes growing bright, even though Nell Stewart was looking at her and Gavin dully. It was as though the girl had come to the end of her resources and could not care what happened to her in the future. In this mood she was dangerous.

Margaret's mind worked swiftly. One other woman, Janet Armstrong, knew the girl was not what she seemed and it was only a matter of time before she ferretted out Nell's true identity. If she asked Janet Armstrong to chaperone Nell, and nursemaid her for the lying-in, that too would solve a problem for her.

"Would ye have Janet Armstrong to nursemaid Lady Helen?" she asked Gavin.

"I would have anything to ease the problem," he said. "I only desire Lady Helen's safety."

"We will ride to Nithrie," Margaret said, decisively, "and take Lady Helen with Janet. We could leave this afternoon and bide the night with Dame Catherine, thy mother, then ride home to Balgennan on the morrow after dawn. I will beg that I must visit my Lady Kennedy over the matter of a new style of gown before the King makes his visit, and beg leave to have thy protection with a few horsemen for the journey. Your absence would be noted, and the Earl would be asking sore questions if you rode to Nithrie with my serving maid and laundry woman, but they can go as my servants. I can find some excuse for leaving them at Nithrie on my return."

Gavin's eyes showed hope.

"Oh, my Lady, you are truly noble," he said. "We will save you yet, my dove," he added, turning to Nell, who stared at him stolidly.

"Why fuss thyself?' she asked tonelessly. "My doom is already writ. Why did I try to evade what lies in my path?"

"Oh cease your haverings," said Margaret, crossly. "I will pack a bag for you of my clothes, and take you to the comfortable home of our good Squire Gavin. He has wronged you, but I have no doubt you asked for it truly. Now I will have a word with Janet Armstrong."

"Not Mistress Armstrong. She is wicked," said Nell.

"Then Dame Catherine can beat the wickedness out of her," said Margaret.

She hurried to find the Earl who was about to preside over a session of complaints from his tenants that afternoon, and to make her request in such a tizzy that he listened to her with half an ear.

"What kind of female pother is this that it cannot wait while we worry about darker deeds?"

"Small pother indeed," she agreed, "but quickly dealt with if Squire Gavin can guard us on our journey now. He will be returned ere time to saddle the horses to ride to Council."

"Be at it then, if you must," said the Earl, peevishly, "but do not linger over gossip." Suddenly his eyes turned shrewd, and he caught Margaret's arm. "I hope this is no ploy of thine, my Lady," he said, sternly. "I'm in no mood for a ploy. There are serious matters of State to consider and other light-skirted affairs can wait."

Margaret's heart almost failed her.

"What . . . what do you mean, my Lord Earl? What light-skirted affair?"

'There is a noisome Fayre near Bargany full of light-headed nonsense like to put serious affairs drifting as on a feather. You are a sensible woman, I grant you, but your youth is still in the turn of your heel and the glint in your eye."

Margaret swallowed. She wanted the task accomplished before Archibald returned from Minnybole where he was on estate duty for the Earl.

"I am a married woman and Mistress of thy household in the absence of wife and Countess. Is it thy true belief that I would go merry-making to a common Fayre?"

The Earl debated, eyeing her thoughtfully as though aware that there was an underlying motive for her visit, but unsure what it could be.

"I take my maid and serving woman," she said steadily.

"Very well, go then, but I expect you back on the morrow, since we ride at noon. See to it."

"Aye, my Lord," she answered, meekly, her cheeks red. It was the first time she had deceived her uncle, and she felt an inward revulsion, as though he could see the lie in her heart. She sent Gavin to receive quick instructions from the Earl and a quick belabouring for allowing himself to get entangled in a woman's ploy, then hurried to seek out Janet Armstrong.

At first the woman looked at her sullenly, but answered with her usual meekness such as she had now adopted, when Margaret put it to her that she go to Nithrie with Nell Stewart.

"The reason need not concern thee," Margaret told her, crisply, "but thy presence at Nithrie is required for as long as is necessary."

"Aye, my Lady.'

"Pack your bag, then, but be quick. The nights draw in early again and we maun be at Nithrie before nightfall. We avoid the Fayre at Bargany and we ride light but strong, and have no wish to be accosted by the revellers."

The woman nodded, though she annoyed Margaret almost into boxing her ears by her taigling, as she slowly bound up her few possessions as though reluctant to be on her way.

It made Margaret all the more determined to have the woman at Nithrie rather than Balgennan, wondering what ploy she had had in mind, if she had remained under the Castle roof. She remembered that the King liked to be approached by the common people to air a grievance, and that he often dispensed justice in kind. Wealthy merchants or burgesses who had been cruel to their underlings, would find themselves stripped to a linen shift and whipped through the streets.

Had Janet Armstrong hoped to petition His Majesty when he walked freely through the Castle keep?

"I will have you beaten if you taigle us the longer," Margaret said, angrily to the woman. "Our party is ready to mount, but for thee."

Lady Nell caught sight of the woman's face as her eyes followed Margaret, and she would fain have dismounted and crawled into some corner of the Castle, well away from Janet Armstrong and the Lady Margaret. Her body felt sick and sore, and her mind too weary for comfort. She was to be married to the Squire, Gavin Johnson, just as soon as he had earned his spurs and came to take over the running of Nithrie from his father, Ninian, who grew frail.

Lady Nell was not sure whether she wanted this marriage or not. Her life had become a mad whirling thing, lived in a twilight world, but there was a certain solace in allowing Lady Margaret to take over. Perhaps there would be love for her at Nithrie. Squire Gavin claimed to have love for her in his heart, but always he was looking over his shoulder in case anyone should hear.

Janet Armstrong was mounted, and Gavin impatient to be away, his head raised to the pale sunshine as though sniffing the air.

" We maun ride apace," he said, spurring his horse, " or twilight will be upon us before we reach Nithrie. Ride tightly, and tidily, and not straggle out along the path, and you . . . you strong-arm men! . . . be ever watchful."

So they set off, and Margaret saw Janet Armstrong turn to look at the old Castle, as she rode away, but there was no sorrow at parting on her face. Rather there was the light of triumph and malevolence in her slanting eyes, and Margaret's heart misgave her. What ailed the woman? Was she glad to be of service to the Johnsons?

Margaret wished she had found some excuse to rid herself of the woman before now, but she was not as ruthless as a man with his enemies, who could force a quarrel and run him through.

As the miles passed and the sky darkened, Margaret began to feel the chill of horror which had assailed her after Elizabeth disappeared, and she saw that the path was beginning to lead them towards the shoreline, and the cold bleak territory which Gavin had shown her on her journey to Balgennan. But she had seen it then on the morning of a warm Spring day, after a good night at the Inn where Elizabeth had last been seen alive. Now it was in the gloaming of a winter's evening, and they would not be staying at the Inn. Instead they would turn off in-country towards Nithrie.

Suddenly the coldness within Margaret gripped her icily, so that she almost cried out, and out of the gloaming she could see the sand dunes crawling with silent shapes of hairy-like animals, their wild cries rending the air as the creatures set upon them.

" Here, Sawney, here! To me! "

Margaret could hear Janet Armstrong's strident voice, and she all but fainted in her saddle as a bright shaft of light from the setting sun showed her a hideous long-haired sinewy figure, with claw-like hands, and a dark, sweating, grinning face staring up at her.

She had ridden into Nightmare.

THIRTEEN

Sir Archibald found the Castle strangely empty when he returned from Minnybole, and went to find Margaret. He had had a good day, managing his affairs with all his old competence and clarity, but he was puzzled to find Margaret and Nell Stewart missing from their quarters. Discussing the business he had transacted in Minnybole with the Earl, he enquired as to where the Lady Margaret had gone.

" To Bargany! " he cried. " What madness is this? Doesn't she know that the Douglases are rising? They are no great friends of ours. They hate the English, and are already looking askance at Margaret. If she meets with a raiding party, then they will have no hesitation in holding her to ransom, and we will be fighting with the Douglases before we know it."

" She is your wife," said the Earl, suddenly realising the truth of the words and that he should have refused permission for her to go on a frivolous ploy.

" I should have thought a son of mine could keep his lady in order."

" That I promise you," said Archibald, grimly. " She is spending no night under Bargan's roof, and she meets the King in rags instead of high fashion, if so be it."

He strode out and re-mounted his horse, calling to his two henchmen who quickly rode by his side. They rode the path already taken by Lady Margaret's party, and Archibald hoped to sight them ahead at each turn of the path, but there was only a few straggling wayfarers.

There was a glow in the sky from the direction of Bargany where a Fayre was being held, and Sir Archibald could have wished himself among the revellers instead of riding with rage in his heart to argue sense into his wife. How much better if they were enjoying themselves watching a dancing bear or a party of gypsy dancers?

Then they were riding into the dark evil-looking territory of high boulders with the sea lashing against the rocky coast, and one of the henchmen cried out as he pointed ahead.

"There's Squire Johnson fechtin' sair, my Lord Archibald. Oh, God save us all, it's the Devil from the Sea!"

"Then we maun poke steel into his black heart," cried Archibald.

"But he divides himself into a hundred pieces," cried the man. "He swarms all over travellers and . . . devours them. We've heard talk of it, and tales to make a stomach turn twice over."

Sir Archibald wasted no time arguing. Somewhere in that swarming throng was his wife, and seconds later he found her, even as a limb of the Devil sought to pull her from her horse. Sir Archibald ran the creature through with his sword, and ordered Margaret to a place of refuge behind a boulder. He saw Gavin Johnson fighting valiantly, and the woman, Armstrong, screeching like an Irish banshee, as though calling the creatures to her, and to do her bidding. Then one of Satan's limbs in female form dragged her off her horse, and several others were on to the woman, who rent the air with her screams that they mistook her for one of the travellers, and they rent her clothing and tore at her belly, and were on to her like ravenous beasts, her blood staining their lips as they fought to quench their thirst, and throw entrails to smaller creatures, clad in hairy ragged clothing, their bodies dark and shining with dirt and sweat.

Their numbers grew and grew, and it was as the henchman had said, that the creature was some sort of Gorgon, multiplying even as they hacked parts of it down.

Sir Archibald quieted the hysterical screechings of Nell Stewart, and ordered her to stay beside Margaret who bravely came out of her shelter to pull Nell behind her and try to quiet her fears, though her own were beyond belief. She found herself lying across her horse, retching, having been powerless to tear her eyes from the horror of watching Janet Armstrong's body being torn apart by the creatures.

Their henchmen were ready to run in fear, and Margaret saw one of them being dragged down, screaming, the creatures at his throat. Sir Archibald and Gavin were fighting bravely though the creatures seemed to leap nimbly aside from each sword thrust, as though not mortal, yet Margaret could see the darkness of blood on the arm of one of the man-like devils, and dashed forward to seize the sword from the henchman who was now sliding from his horse, even as he let it go.

" Stay in thy refuge," roared Archibald. " Do as I tell thee, my Lady. I will deal with thee later."

" I fight by thy side," she said, cutting about her with the heavy blade. " I have no precious life to preserve like Lady Helen, but mine own. These creatures are human and not immortal. They bleed and fall like ourselves. They are no supernatural beings."

Suddenly they could hear faint sounds of revelry which grew ever louder, and Sir Archibald shouted to Gavin.

" There is a party of men coming from beyond that rock, on their way homeward from the Fayre at Bargany. We maun pray they are merry enough for further sport to hunt these creatures."

The creatures were already aware of the crowds from the Fayre, and suddenly they were calling out instructions to one another in guttural Scots, and gathering their wounded to them, even as Gavin and Archibald still fought them off.

Then the revellers were upon them, while the creatures seemed to swarm towards the sea, and Sir Archibald explained to the leading members of the party, young healthy freemen and burgesses from Galloway, what had happened, and pointed to the sight of the hairy creatures vanishing over the sands towards the sea, and sobering the heads of the party. Janet Armstrong lay dead, her body and clothing darkly stained, as did two of the henchmen, but none of the creatures even though several had been wounded.

No wonder they had never been found before, thought

Archibald, since they were well disciplined into picking up dead and wounded. They would have carried Janet and their two men with them, if the revellers had not come upon them so quickly. There would have been no evidence to show that they had ever been there, except for blood on the sands, and the footprints washed away when the tide came in. But for the revellers, they would all have been overcome in time.

"We return to Balgennan," said Sir Archibald, after he had taken the names and learned where to find the revellers, making them swear to bear witness against what they had seen. He had no doubt it was a case for High Court and the Magistrates in Glasgow, or even Edinburgh.

"These creatures must be found," he said, sternly. "Too many wayfarers have vanished and it could be your turn next gan we do not smoke them out, and deal with them. You can reflect in your heads whether to speak out and with a true tongue, or have it cut out with my sword for craven cowards. But if you speak out, then Balgennan will not be without gratitude. Already we bear losses to the creatures. So swear on it."

"That we swear," cried the ringleader, an upstanding young man, son of a Galloway merchant, "and right gladly. My father lost a brother a year gone, and blamed the Innkeeper further up the coast, seeing the man hanged, though it wad seem the man was innocent. It is my debt to put the case to rights. Aye, I will swear, my Lord. And so will the rest of us, if something be done about compensation for the poor innocents unjustly punished."

"So be it," said Sir Archibald. "Go thy way, and God care for thee. We are in your debt, and owe you our lives."

Squire Gavin had lifted Nell Stewart's trembling body on to his horse, holding her in his arms. She was making low moaning noises and he was trying to comfort her.

Sir Archibald called to their henchmen who were used to battle, but were now almost stiff with fright.

"Must I run all of you through for cowardice?" he cried. "Come! To horse, and ride behind if you would prefer a woman to protect you. The Lady Margaret rides beside me."

Sick with shame and fright, they formed a group, their clothing torn and their flesh bleeding from deep scratches. They had covered up the bodies of Janet Armstrong and their two companions in a sheltered place against returning in the morning. They were too worn and spent, and sick with pain and fright to carry them home this night.

*   *   *

The Earl was irritated by the waywardness of the younger generation of his household, rendered all the more annoying since he could not give vent to his wrath and allow the Castle to resound to his roars, indulged in rarely, but all the more terrifying for that.

An hour before, the King's Messenger had again ridden into the courtyard, bearing a message to say that His Majesty was resting at Ayr, but would be riding into Balgennan within the hour, accompanied only by one or two courtiers and a band of soldiers, as he was wont to do at times, when making a private visit.

The matter of Paul Crawar had been dealt with speedily, the man having made no attempt to deny his guilt, but seemed to relish his martyrdom, believing that it would open the minds of the people to the doctrines he had preached, and show them the more clearly that Christendom of the present day was far removed from the gentle goodness preached by Jesus Christ to his followers.

The King had signed the warrant condemning him to be burned, and felt weary of looking on death when he was not sure in his heart that the deed was foul enough for such punishment.

Now he had decided to keep to his plans and visit his lands in the south-west of the Kingdom, with a stern eye towards Douglas who was ever zealous in fighting the English, but who was growing almost as powerful as the King, himself.

Sir Thomas was proud to entertain his King, but he fretted and fumed at the absence of Lady Margaret, not to mention his son, Sir Archibald, choosing to ride after her to bring her back to Balgennan. Young people today, the Earl reflected, were made of soft stuff, not like in his day when a threat of a day in the dungeons would soon have him minding his business.

Luckily the arrangements Lady Margaret had already made kept the panics from sending everything into a state of chaos, though the well-ordered, smooth-running of the household was absent, and the Earl was finding himself enraged at the absence of the Mistress of his household, not to mention his son and the Squire.

The King loved good food and the richness of his office, but he had never removed himself from the realities of life for the common people. Now he had thrown himself into a chair in front of a great fire of logs and coal, which blazed in the wide fireplace in the Great Hall. He was used to hustle and bustle and saw nothing wrong with his welcome.

"I have been weary in the saddle, Sir Thomas," he confessed. "I am glad to shed heavy garments before this good fire, and rest before I dine. Some days go ill with me."

Some days went ill with him too, thought the Earl!

"My pleasure is thy comfort, Sire, and 'tis my hope that my poor table satisfies thy needs."

"Ah well, my needs are satisfied easily. Other things trouble me more. I mislike the burning of the heretic, Sir Thomas, though the man spread his poison ere he was caught. We cannot burn the ears of his listeners. As a boy, imprisoned at the English Court, I read the works of John Wycliffe, and the years have served to show him as a dangerous thinker, and we maun burn other heretics, but the seeds planted in men's minds will take root and grow."

"I have not read the works you mention, Sire, but I hope I am loyal to our Church."

"Aye, and thousands like thee, good Sir Thomas, who are loyal without question," he said. "But Wycliffe saw the Church as a community of believers rather than the ecclesiastical hierarchy, and he had a powerful friend in John o' Gaunt, or he would maybe have suffered the same fate as poor Crawar. Mind you, the Clergy have not been idle and the movements like the Hussites have not got the hold on the people I had feared, though at times I felt unease and wondered if the roots be spreading under the soil. The danger seemed to me, that it was coming from intellectual minds, originating in Oxford . . . Wycliffe to begin with, and more recently a man called Payne. But Crawar is but a poor man . . ."

" A physician," said Sir Thomas, unthinkingly, and the King frowned.

" You have met this man, Balgennan?"

Sir Thomas' honest face flushed.

" He attended my son who was sick of his wounds. He came here as a physician, not as a preacher. I acknowledged his skill in medicine, but cannot acknowledge his teaching of religion, since I heard none."

" You are fortunate," said the King, coolly. " Most of the heretics are unskilled and untaught in what they preach, and they would destroy without the skill to build. That is why I concur in repressing them and signing the warrant for Crawar. I had thought the English Court unenvied in dealing with the unrest it stirs up, but now we maun keep our eyes open before it spreads throughout our Kingdom.

" There has been much that is wrong with the Holy Church, but I counselled the Clergy to right themselves from within and root out their own corruption, and will try to keep the silk-tongued critic from leaving destruction behind him, with no Holy place of purity and perfection ready to sit on the site."

" No Sire," Sir Thomas agreed, though his mind was only half on what the King was saying. Rather he was turning over the hospitality his servants had been set to arrange.

" The Douglases grow restive for a plunder into England," mused the King, reaching out to stir a log with his foot, and settle himself into even further comfort. " It is ever so, baiting the English. Not that they don't deserve it, since a map shows clearly where the Border should be drawn and that Cumberland and most of Northumberland is part of our Kingdom. But for the nonce we live in peace with our neighbours, and

I am already well ahead in plans to make our Kingdom a sweet one to be envied.

"I feel weary in my spirit at times, but I see great things to be done with our heritage. We could grow rich by selling our goods to foreign countries, such as Italy, as Aeneas Sylvius showed me, even as we do by selling our hides and wool to Flanders. We might even trade with England, if the Border clans forget their differences. I have heard from the mouth of Aeneas that the Italians like the wool cloth from England, and that they are calling with ships to a place in the South coast of England . . . South Hampton . . . to collect the wool cloth, even as they do from Flanders. We find that Flanders admires our pearls from the rivers, and Italy is a dainty land and admiring of pearls. We would do well to trade with Italy, and become rich and gracious of living.

"But I see thee are restless of my chatter, Sir Thomas. Perhaps you are one of those thinking that true riches are gained in battle, along with fine honours. It could be that you are right, Sir Thomas. The English Court resounded with pride and conceit when King Henry V ruled France, though he ruled that country when it was divided within itself, and found it easy to gain power over it. Now I see the French gathering themselves to throw off the English yoke. They will not hold France any more than they will hold Scotland, but we maun learn a lesson from our neighbours, Sir Thomas. We maun unite, and build universities for true education of our children, so that they have more in their heads than putting their neighbours to the sword.

"Our skills could feed our poor, but always the powerful maun be yet more powerful, and the rich yet more rich, to their own ends. I grow weary with their lack of sense."

Suddenly there was a disturbance and the sound of raised voices from the direction of the stairs which led from the courtyard up to the Great Hall, and Sir Thomas turned, half in relief, and then in alarm as Sir Archibald and Squire Gavin appeared in the Hall, supporting Lady Margaret and Nell Stewart, whose gowns were spattered with blood.

"Great Heavens, have ye no sense o' decency?" he bawled,

forgetting in his anger and fright that his King was a guest in his household, and had risen to stand beside him, his fingers automatically feeling for the sword which he had now laid aside.

"My apologies, my Lord," said Sir Archibald, quickly stepping forward, followed by Gavin and Margaret.

Quickly they made their obeisance to the King, though Nell Stewart stood like an automaton, her unblinking eyes on the man who had destroyed her family.

"We have uncovered the Galloway beast who destroys travellers and wayfarers," said Sir Archibald, quickly, "but we maun return to seek him out of his lair, as soon as day breaks. He is Satan divided into many limbs, who set upon us and devoured Lady Margaret's woman servant by tooth and claw . . ."

"Cease thy haverings," thundered Sir Thomas. "Where is thy courtesy to thy Liege Lord, who is a guest in our Household? Thy wife could be better employed in harrying the servants into proper hospitality than cavorting about the countryside . . ."

Lady Margaret turned pale, and again curtseyed low to the King, and asked pardon to return to her duties.

But James was ever intrigued by the smallest happening in his Kingdom, and he commanded the two young men to tell him the story in detail. He had been aware of the poor reputation of Innkeepers on the South-west coast, and had signed a warrant for the hanging of more than one against the destruction of wayfarers who were last seen at their Inn.

Lady Margaret begged leave, again, to go to her room with her maid and supervise the King's table, and when it was granted, she hustled Nell Stewart to their chambers, up the spiral staircase, and quickly stripped the girl of her clothing, then dozed her with physic, and put her to bed.

"If you let a moan slip from your lips to the ears of the King, I shall push a knife in thy ribs," she threatened, then put her own head between her knees against a faint. She must be strong to see that the King had comfort and hospitality, thankful that he was only riding with a company of Household guards and one or two courtiers, and not the Queen and her children, who were at Linlithgow.

"Have you marked the spot well where the Devil holds his foul ritual?" the King was asking.

"Aye, Sire, we have indeed," Sir Archibald assured him, earnestly. "We maun go back to bury our dead who are hidden there against the light of day. We could not bring their bodies home without ill to our own persons."

"Then tomorrow we take my men and lift Satan from his den, limb by limb," said James, his eyes shining. "It will be greater sport than the Wolves or the Stags."

Sir Thomas' face was red unto bursting. He had never heard such a preposterous story. No sooner had the last of His Majesty's horsemen ridden out of the yett, then he would given his son and his squire something to remember the visit by. A spell in the dungeons was too lenient for them!

"We give thee leave to clean up thy persons," said the King, "and the good Sir Thomas and Lady Margaret conduct us to our meal, then we will eat and drink, then rest our limbs, and we ride at dawn. How say you, Sir Thomas?"

"Very well, Sire."

But although the Earl might have been proud of his table in other conditions, and pleased with Lady Margaret, he sat solemnly through the meal, then had a quiet word with his son, and Squire, before retiring.

"'Fore God, I ought to break your head, Sir," he told Archibald, "to shame our House in front of our lawful Monarch. What fool ploy do thee offer the King?"

"No mad ploy, Sir," said Archibald, earnestly. "The creatures ate the entrails of thy servant, Janet Armstrong. Her body lies waiting burial near the rocky Galloway coast, and two of our henchmen."

Sir Thomas paused. Janet Armstrong had given him solace at one time when he had none, though she had been no sweet maid. She had been a woman of strange depths, and some said witch. Perhaps she had conjured up the Devil's brood such as they claimed. If the King should find out his connection with her, there would be no end to his shame.

" Fools! " he said, straining to keep his voice low. " If thee bring more shame to Balgennan, then a spell in the dungeons will teach thee sense. As for my Squire, I give you leave to retire to Nithrie, gan His Majesty leave for Threave. Some other master can have the training of thee. I shall send a message to your father, my kinsman Ninian, and Dame Catherine, thy mother."

Gavin swallowed and bowed. So he had gained nothing, not even his spurs, nor yet his wife. Instead of being safe at Nithrie, Nell Stewart lay upstairs, asleep of a potion given by Lady Margaret, yet no distance from the King's own quarters. What if the Earl knew that she was from Albany's family, and that she was with child by him?

He lay down on his cot with an aching head, dried blood having crusted behind his ear from the talons of one of the creatures, though at last exhaustion drove him to sleep.

Then the bagpipes were sounding, and it was time to rise and start the day with assembly for prayers. Gavin rolled, heavy-eyed, from his bed and went to put his head in a bowl of water. He would need it free of cobwebs for the day.

FOURTEEN

Lady Margaret provided breakfast for the King, his courtiers and his armed men, though members of her own Household had little appetite for breakfast. Sir Archibald looked as pale as he had done during his illness, and Gavin was even more heavy-eyed. The Earl's face was hard and cold, his eyes promising retribution if they were about to embark on needless business.

When all the horsemen were assembled in the Courtyard, the Earl was again enraged to see Lady Margaret, in riding dress, about to ride out beside her husband.

"Have ye no sense, Mistress?" he bawled, and the King rode forward and reined in beside him, though the Earl was too angry to care. "Return to thy spinning and thy stitching, woman, and care for our Household. Do you think you are a *man*?"

Lady Margaret's colour was high.

"My Lord, I have been witness to the deeds we go to uncover. My serving maid lies dead, hidden by the rocks, and my sister was victim to this terrible creature. My Lord, I pray your indulgence, and your consent to my presence at my husband's side."

The King nodded and made a sign to the Earl, who sulkily gave her leave to ride behind Sir Archibald and Gavin.

It was a fair distance riding to the Galloway coastline, and Margaret felt no joy in watching the dawn breaking behind the distinctive outline of the mountains of Arran, with the stronghold of Ailsa Craig rearing out of the sea. There was little wind, but the morning was dull and cold, and she pulled the hood of her cloak closer about her ears, as they followed

154

the path they had taken, in much higher spirits, the previous day.

After an hour or two's riding, Sir Archibald's face grew pale and tense, as Gavin rode up to join him. Sir Archibald turned to the King.

" Sire, we ride near the spot where we were attacked, and where the murdered woman and two men lie hidden."

" Find the bodies that we may examine them," the King ordered, crisply. " I would see the condition of the woman, such as is thy description of the matter."

Sir Archibald and Gavin dismounted, while the King gave the order for their party of horsemen to rein in, then the two young men hurried to look behind the boulders, only to return shortly afterwards.

" The . . . the bodies have gone, Sire," said Sir Archibald, worriedly.

" Let me look! " cried Margaret, and she, too, walked forward, searching frantically while the Earl seemed to be carved from stone. The tide had been in, washing all the evidence, but Archibald prowled round, even as Margaret returned with a small piece of brown wool cloth.

" This is from the cloak of my maidservant, Sire," she said. " It was caught on the rock."

" We have the names and addresses of witnesses from Galloway who saw the creatures. They are men of character and honesty, Sire."

The King's eyes were scanning the area with keen observation, looking down on the rocky coastline where the sea could lash itself to a frenzy against the rocks with boiling foam, though this morning it was gentle, though dully grey.

" The creatures went seawards? " he asked Gavin.

" Aye, Sire, and in past days there has been blood on the sands and the footprints as of a child. Some of the creatures were of a small size, Your Majesty."

The King seemed to grow in stature as he marshalled his men and commanded them to hunt the area, apportioning the soldiers so that every rock and sandbank would be examined as far as the shoreline.

Gavin had taken the piece of brown wool from Lady Margaret, examining it closely, and sniffing its odour.

"If it pleases Your Majesty," he said, going forward to bow again to the King, "my poor homestead lies near at hand, and my father owns bloodhounds. The dogs would smell out the path which the creatures took to the sea, if they carried the woman with them, as must have happened. This piece of wool would give them the scent."

"See to it, Squire," the King commanded, his eyes bright and keen, and Gavin bowed and quickly mounted his horse, promising to return within the hour.

The Earl looked at him balefully as he rode towards the path which turned off for Nithrie, and Gavin's heart sank. Soon he would be back to Nithrie, the past three years washed away as though they had never been. He would return in disgrace and may not even manage to take Nell Stewart as his bride.

He had visited his old home but rarely over the past three years, and when he rode into the courtyard of the old house which was little more than a farmstead, the household was well astir, and the servants going about their affairs.

His father, Master Ninian Johnson, had ridden to consult with a miller over the supply of grain, but his mother, Dame Catherine, clad in white linen, was baking pies. She almost pulled Gavin from his horse with glad cries, thinking he was already returned with his knighthood and a parchment for extra land.

"I ride swiftly gan the King and his men are waiting on the shore," he told her. "There is little time to tell thee more, but I need the bloodhounds to smell out the sea creatures . . ."

The Dame turned pale.

"Do not touch that evil," she said, urgently. "It will attack thee and despoil thy good fortune."

"It is despoiled already," groaned Gavin, "but I have no time to tell thee the tale. My mother, if I should return to Nithrie with a maid whom I would fain wed, will thee take her into thy household, and protection? She bears my child."

" What folly is this?" cried the Dame. " Has thee been dallying with a light-skirt?"

" No light-skirt. She is a lady born."

"Then what say her family?"

" She has no family. I cannot tell thee everything. It would take too long."

He was harnessing the bloodhounds who were straining to go, and Dame Catherine was staring at him with a worried face, wanting to question him for an hour or yet longer, but recognising that His Majesty must not be kept waiting. She would fain have gone with Gavin, having never set eyes on her King, but she had dread of his present location.

" I shall tell you more when the dogs are returned," Gavin promised, kissing his mother's plump cheek, then he set off back down the trail towards the coastline, the dogs howling by his side.

The soldiers had found nothing, and there was no movement along the shoreline except for the swift flight of the gulls, and the sough of the sea as it dashed against the cliffs and gently rolled into small caverns.

" There is nothing to be found," said Sir Archibald bitterly, when Gavin returned. " The creature must not be of human flesh and blood. Only Satan's evil sorcery could vanish all the evidence of the horror we witnessed."

" What say you now, Squire?" the King was asking, as he searched the area keenly, and rode up again to the young men. Gavin was offering the scrap of wool to the dogs to sniff, then they began to renew their howling, making Lady Margaret pull her cloak about her against the chill and desolation of those howls.

Then the dogs surged forward towards the sea, smelling and stopping to sniff again, the scent faint except in some parts where they had dragged Janet Armstrong in her cloak after the washings from the sea.

Soon Squire Gavin and Sir Archibald were following on foot, while the King commanded his men to keep pace with them, as they disappeared down a rough path and almost plunged into the sea, then turned back along a sandy path which skirted a foaming caldon of sea in the cavern.

Sir Archibald was hardly aware of the man behind him, or of his wife picking up her skirts and treading the sandy wet path, her shoes softened and ruined by the sea water. The dogs were uttering weird howls and fighting to go forward into inner caverns.

"We need torches," cried Archibald and Squire Gavin threw the command behind him, so that Margaret heard it echoed among the henchmen. Soon the torches were lit and passed forward to throw light on the caverns and show them the way.

The ground grew dry and solid under their feet, and they were walking towards an inner chamber, then the full horror of the creatures they had come to find was upon them.

Later Margaret thought that her principal sensation was of walking into Hell. As the dogs leapt ahead along passages which had been hewn out and wound in and out like a maze, then opened out into a large chamber, she could feel the great chill of sickness and fear take hold of her body as never before. They were into a chamber, and there was a stench enough to falter the hearts of Sir Archibald and Squire Gavin who led the party, hardened though they were to brutal scenes in battle.

But the dogs were howling hideously, and behind they could hear the King and his party of soldiers.

"My father was right," he growled. "This is no place for a woman. 'Tis time your strong-headed ways were mended, Madam, and I shall see that they are gan we emerge unscathed from this descent into Hell."

"My feet will save thee the trouble," said Margaret, her teeth chattering. "They support an old woman, not the young maid who married thee."

Then as the torches began to bring more light, and the King, with his men, began to fill the cavern, there was no room for more words, and for a long time the only sound was the hideous baying of the dogs who had the foulest creatures ever seen at their mercy.

The cave was huge, with an upper gallery and a round

framework in the centre filled with dry wood and sea coal, ready to light. They were night creatures and had been sleeping, since it was day.

The King ordered a soldier to set alight to the wood, and as it blazed up, the chamber was lighted and Margaret felt Sir Archibald's arm drawing her ever close as they stared at the creatures who numbered around fifty. They were headed by a huge old man with matted grey hair and his wife, who was staring at Margaret with a wolfish grin, which showed only two long yellowed teeth. Ranged round them were younger men and women, shining with sweat and filth, some with young children at their feet or breast.

Hanging from the ceiling in rows, like the hams in her kitchen, Margaret felt sickness sweeping over her as she looked upon rows and rows of human limbs, arms, legs and various other dismembered sections of human bodies. There were also great tubs of pickling brine, and Margaret's stomach revolted, but not before she saw that it held a similar collection.

On another side of the cave the creatures had made their store house, and she could see great quantities of clothes, some poor homespun and some rich silks and velvets such as her sister had worn. Other piles of money, precious jewellery and fine weapons were laid out, the spoils of a quarter of a century.

Then the creatures sent up their banshee wailings to add to the moans of the dogs, and would have rushed at their throats except that the dogs held them at bay, and the King shouted loudly in command.

"That this . . . *this* could happen in my Kingdom," said King James. "But for thy son, Balgennan, and his lady, and the Squire, I would have misdoubted any evidence but that of my own eyes. We have enough men to marshal the creatures. They are to be confined to the Tolbooth in Edinburgh. I will give orders that these . . . what's left of God's poor creatures and my subjects . . . be buried decently in the sands, and the plunder be brought to Edinburgh, as evidence to the Magistrates."

*   *   *

It was a day when every minute seemed like an hour to Margaret, and every hour a day, as the soldiers marshalled the creatures, and the old man and woman were questioned, on behalf of the King. At first it hardly seemed possible that they could speak, so like to devilish creatures they were, but soon they were all yelling and talking in the thick guttural tongue of the common language such as Margaret found difficult to understand.

" So thy name be Sawney Bean," the man was asked, " and this woman thy wife, or common-law wife?"

" Aye," growled the man. " My wife."

" How come thee here? Are thee product of an older generation living on yonder cave?"

The questions went on and on. The man had been born in East Lothian, eight miles east of Edinburgh, and he had been brought up by his father to follow his own employment as a hedger and ditcher.

" Thee were brought up to honest employment," said the courtier who asked the questions. " Your belly was filled, yet you must leave your father and mother to come here to rob and plunder, and hide your spoils in a cave. Robbing and murder only brought coins and jewels and clothing such as you could not eat, nor could you spend the money against fear of discovery. So you ate your victims."

The woman gave a harsh cackle of laughter, her yellow teeth gleaming. It was easy to see where the cannibalism had started.

The other creatures began to be segregated and counted, eight sons, six daughters, eighteen grandsons, fourteen grand-daughters, all born of incest.

Margaret's eyes were on the smallest of the creatures as they were seared into her memory. She thought of the limbs she and Sir Archibald had seen washed up on the shore near Balgennan. Now it was easy to see where they had come from. No traveller had been allowed to go their way, to tell their tale in years gone by. It was only in recent times that their numbers had grown larger, and therefore less tight and careful, though the man such as the henchmen from Elizabeth's party, had been unable to tell, his head being cleaved and his brain fevered by the sight.

But Janet Armstrong had known, thought Margaret, and had sought to deliver them into Sawney Bean's hands in her hatred of Margaret who stood in her way of gaining influence over the Earl once more. Yet the creatures, on night plunder, had not stopped to distinguish friend or foe, nor could there be belief in having friends. Perhaps Janet Armstrong, through her witchcraft, had come upon Sawney Bean at some time, and had made some sort of agreement. But she had paid the penalty.

* * *

The King was pleased with the Earl's young Squire, whose bloodhounds had found the inner cave for them, and he said so at the end of the day, asking Gavin to kneel before him while he knighted him in time-honoured tradition, and granted further acres to swell his Barony.

" I am well pleased with you," he said, now that the gang were on their way to the Tolbooth, and the King and his men about to depart for Edinburgh, his plans changed yet again, but he must see that the gang got their deserts. He was, in fact, giving the whole matter first priority, but he thanked the Earl for his hospitality, be it short-lived.

" It is a sweet Earldom," he said, drawing in deep breaths of good sea air, and looking out on the lovely view across the Firth of Clyde to Arran and the Mull beyond. " It will be all the sweeter for having thy coastline swept clean of such foul sins."

Now he was smiling benevolently on Sir Archibald and Gavin, well pleased to see that gallantry and initiative was well to the fore in the younger generation of knights.

" Now you must find yourself a wife," he counselled Gavin, " and set about cultivating thy Barony, to the benefit of our

Kingdom. Ah . . . I see you are not blate about it. Is thy lass of good standing to do thee credit?"

" B . . . beyond my standing, Sir," mumbled Gavin, never able to prevaricate.

" And her guardians protecting her from a humble Squire, I don't doubt," said the King, knowingly. " But the King can give permission for a match if he be satisfied it is a noble one. Come now, Sir Gavin, who is the lady, and I will attend to it as an extra prize. I am well pleased with you."

Gavin swallowed, his cheeks crimson, while Sir Archibald and Margaret looked on rooted in fear. The Earl was smiling benignly, pleased that his household had been of such help in finally solving an age-old mystery, and rooting out the fear of supernatural evil.

" Speak up, lad," he ordered Gavin.

" It . . . it's the Lady Helen Stewart," stuttered Gavin, " grand-daughter to . . . to . . . Albany . . ."

The King's face went wooden, his eyes seemed to start out of his head.

" What nonsense is this?" asked the Earl. " Where is the wench?"

" She lives here, in this household," said Gavin eagerly, now that the first push had been made. With the King's permission to marry, and his new Barony, he could not see beyond the fact that all his problems were about to be solved.

" The lad's brain has been turned," thundered the Earl. " Albany's maid! . . . beneath my roof! . . . I've never heard of such a nightmare."

His voice rang with sincerity and the King looked at him, his keen eyes going back to the boy, whose white face as he looked at the Earl seemed like to corroborate his statement. The maid had no doubt been kept under the Earl's nose without his permission.

" One apple, even small but rotten, can ruin the barrel," he said slowly. " We will talk about this another time, Sir Gavin, and you too, Balgennan. Rest after this day's labours, then we will get to the roots of these hallucinations, if hallucinations they be. Where is Sir Archibald and his lady?"

He looked round, and the two young people walked forward wearily, hardly daring to look at one another, or the Earl.

"You will both be called before the Magistrates to swear witness against Sawney Bean and his gang of cutthroats, and worse . . . though thy testimony will be simple. The creatures will condemn themselves, but I want everyone in my Kingdom to know that they are discovered, and trailed out of their den, none being left. New trees grown from such poisoned seed will, themselves, produce poisoned fruit."

His eyes were again on Sir Gavin whose body seemed like to drop at the blow of a feather.

"So be it. We deal with Sawney Bean, then we will see if the sickness in the boy's head be cured by sleep or if it be of lasting merit."

"Your servant, Sire," said the Earl, bowing, while they all followed suit, with Margaret bobbing a low curtsey. Then the horsemen were riding out of the courtyard, through the yett and over the drawbridge.

Gavin's sickness enveloped him and he sunk to the floor, where Margaret quickly gave orders to carry him to bed.

"This hour tomorrow we will talk of this day's events," said the Earl, "and the brain fever assailing Sir Gavin. He is out of his head, but I maun find out what put the humours there in the first place."

"We will talk then," agreed Sir Archibald, quietly, and took Margaret's hand, calling to a maid to help her to their quarters, where Nell Stewart still lay in a stupor. Margaret's draught had not been mixed with a light hand, she thought, looking at the sleeping girl, but she had used a potion which could do no more than bring refreshing sleep.

"I will not leave you alone," said Sir Archibald, "but we bed together to comfort one another."

"I want no such comfort," said Margaret, "but beg leave to be given my own company such as I've always had in this chamber. Did ye not see the children of those foul creatures, born of union with brother and sister? Did ye not see what nature of animal they produced, one with another? Do you not forget that we are cousins, and that your father was brother to my own mother?"

"I see no comparison," said Archibald. "It is a common thing for cousins to marry. Do you think we turn our children cannibal?"

"Do not pretend stupidity and no understanding. You know full well what I am trying to say. We maun get dispensation, and thank God we have not yet joined in union."

Sir Archibald's face turned red, and he caught her hand.

"It is only the fears and horrors of the cave which put these notions in your head. Sleep on it, my wife, and you will see that your tongue speaks from a fevered mind. Dose yourself with a potion such as you have given poor Nell Stewart and refresh yourself so that the cobwebs clear from your head. I will not force you . . . this time."

She went into her chamber, and closed the door.

FIFTEEN

The Earl of Balgennan was a worried man, too worried almost for rage against his family, as he gazed into Nell Stewart's pale face, knowing now that the young maidservant was, in truth, a member of the Albany family.

"It maun please you to know," he told his son, "that our House is all but ruined. The King is a stern man and demands utter obedience, and he gets it by dealing through example with those who disobey him. We could be thrown into prison, all of us, and Balgennan lands taken by the Crown.

"It will be no hardship to His Majesty to confiscate our lands, since he finds them fair to look upon, and especially now that the evil has gone. He would find the sea air fresh and pure for his children."

"Surely he would not punish so severely," cried Lady Margaret. "He is also a fair Knight, sworn to chivalry, and the protection of his ladies, and Lady Helen is his own kinswoman."

"For any other family he could, in truth, be prevailed upon, but not for Albany's, who made no attempt to rescue him while he was being held to ransom at the English Court, even though Duke Murdoch, himself a prisoner of Northumberland, at the same time James was held in London, was soon exchanged for the son of Percy. They had put themselves above the Crown."

He turned scornfully to Sir Gavin.

"Do you think that this maiden would have listened to you, or stepped near your path, if her father had still been in power? Nay, her lofty instep would have walked on palace floors, wearing satin slippers."

" I pity her," said Margaret. " She has lost her home, her people, her lands, her honour, and has had her life threatened many times . . ."

" Cease thy haverings, woman," said the Earl, sourly. " I am not pleased with thee."

" She defends me, not the Lady Helen," said Sir Archibald, stepping forward. " It is I who brought Lady Helen Stewart to Balgennan, and would have wed her a year ago had the King not made his will known so harshly.

" Lady Helen escaped her destruction through the good offices of Graham, and I took charge of her since the King's eye was ever on Sir Robert, keeking to see his intentions."

" He is no friend to the King."

" Would you be friend to the King if he puts us in prison, just because I helped Nell Stewart? Will he accept your word that the girl was unknown to you? Will your years of service stand you in good stead, or will it serve you nought?"

" I do not know," said the Earl, wearily. " We could have conducted her to the home of my sister, Lady Mary, since her daughter here is so sure that she would welcome the girl, but for this oaf of the loose tongue, he that has now title and land, though there has never been a time when he deserved it less."

Sir Gavin's face was scarlet, but he, too, came to stand guard over Nell.

" My Lord Earl, I have served you well, as has been acknowledged many times. I have gone out and fought for you, cared for your sword, shielded your life with my own, and honoured your house when I would fain have wrecked it over my lady. I did not seek the love of Lady Helen, but it came upon me and would make a lion of me in her defence. But for the monsters, now on their way to Edinburgh, she would be in the arms of my mother Dame Catherine. A poor Barony is better than a rich grave, and I offer that poor Barony. Already she bears my child . . ."

" Is there no end to his infamy?" asked the Earl. " To seduce the girl under my roof!"

" I ask leave to take my Lady to Nithrie," said Sir Gavin,

white-faced, but still brave, "and there I shall call on the priest to wed us. By law she is of age."

"But of royal blood. She would need the King's consent."

"She is of no blood but her own, since if it were royal, it would be spilled. The priest shall not know her identity, and we will have the knot tied 'fore God, if not 'fore the King."

The Earl looked as though he had heard enough.

"Take her, then, to Dame Catherine, and take her now, since you be called to Edinburgh as witness with the rest of us. Your choice of wife makes your new Barony rest lightly on your head, Sir Gavin. I wish you joy, though you may have ruined us all."

Sir Gavin bowed, and took Nell Stewart's hand.

"Come, Lady Helen," he said gently. "This time we ride openly and freely. The terror of the sands has gone, and my mother's arms await thee, as I know having told her when I returned my father's bloodhounds. She has room in her heart for another fine daughter, and a grandson in time."

She drew back, cringeing from him, her face crumpling and Margaret put an arm round her.

"Come now, Lady Nell, I will find you a sonsy maid to your service and you will ride to safety. Sir Gavin will be a fine husband and love thee well."

"Love," repeated Nell, dully. "Love me well. What is love?"

"I will return the horses when I accompany you to Edinburgh, my Lord Earl," said Gavin, bowing formally.

"Oh, get thee hence, lad. Take all for your needs and . . . and a purse for your wedding, though it shows fit to be celebrated in doom."

*　　　*　　　*

The Castle was shrouded in mists rolling in from the sea when Sir Gavin rode out, yet once again, with Nell Stewart by his side. This journey, in spite of the dampness and the cold, gave him sweeter air to breathe as they touched the Galloway coast, then turned inland for Nithrie. Already he could feel the lightening of oppression as of a wound lanced and ready to heal.

The old farmhouse of Nithrie was full of sweet spicy smells, and was rich with baking, when Sir Gavin lifted Nell Stewart into his arms, and carried her into his home, while his mother ran towards them, and his father's bluff welcome rang in his ears.

" This is the maid I maun wed," Sir Gavin told the Dame. " Deal lightly with her, my mother. She has faced more terrors than you have in a lifetime of nightmares. She has suffered enough to turn the minds of six females."

The Dame looked at Nell's white face and tortured eyes.

" Ah, my poor bairn," she said, holding out her strong plump arms. " We will send for the priest to make you my true daughter, and I will care for thee, my love. Your time will soon be upon you, but it will mean great happiness for us all at Nithrie. Rest well and forget your fears. Your bed will be soft and will keep out the chill winds, from whatever direction they blow."

Nell Stewart's small face crumpled, and she was gathered to Dame Catherine's warm bosom, where she wept out her terrors, and her desolation.

" I thought love had gone from this earth," she said. " I thought only to see pain and death."

" If ye seek love, then it flows richly at Nithrie. We are not grand, but we are comfortable, and even the servants are plump with content. Come, let us wash away the dust of the journey, and comb your pretty hair, then feed you with due nourishment."

Sir Gavin looked at his father gravely, when they had gone.

" There may be troubled times ahead for us here," he said, " I have displeased the King."

" Yet he has given you lands, and we are now a Barony . . ."

" I displeased him later. My new lands are as slippery as wet moss on the stepping stones."

Quickly he told the Master of Nithrie what had transpired, and watched the shadows gather on his father's face.

" The King has doubtful humours," he agreed, " but your service in clearing out the Galloway cesspit of Sawney Bean and his gang may weigh in your favour. Half the Kingdom will look on their trial, and the fears of supernatural devilry in that area have spread far and wide. The people will ever rejoice to have the cesspit cleaned out, and many will sleep easier in their beds of a night than they have done since birth."

" It could be so," Gavin agreed, though neither he nor Master Ninian rejoiced whole-heartedly. The future was not as bright as the Dame's smile.

SIXTEEN

The whole countryside had turned out to watch Sawney Bean and his tribe as they were marched along the route to Edinburgh, strongly guarded by the King's soldiers who ever prodded them into obedience as they glared and spat at the onlookers who had never seen such a sight.

Some of the people who had lost members of their family without trace, took up stones to throw, but the armed men gave due warning since the stones could have hit the guard and caused disruption enough to allow even one of the gang to escape.

As news of the march spread, the route was ever more lined with spectators, rich and poor alike, who were horrified, sickened or entertained according to their nature, though the armed men were thankful to arrive at the Tolbooth, and to count that the numbers were correct, forty-eight in all.

The stench of their bodies and repulsive appearance was enough to test the strongest of stomachs and they were not sorry to have the gang behind bars.

*   *   *

The Earl, Archibald and Margaret, followed by Gavin and other witnesses from Balgennan and Galloway rode into Edinburgh the following morning. It was a silent party, thought Margaret, remembering her excitement and interest on their previous visit. This time there would be no merry-making, but the ordeal of swearing against a loathsome group of people, yet Lady Margaret held herself tightly, and knew she would not falter in courage, remembering her sister, and knowing her fate and that of Bessie Laird.

On reaching Court, she was more than relieved to find that the King had decreed that any process of trial of the creatures would be a mockery, and a waste of time. They could not deny their guilt, since His Majesty had been himself present when their den had been discovered, and all the plunder they had stored up over the past quarter of a century bore silent testimony to the fate of many a traveller.

He called forth the Earl of Balgennan and his Household to be simple about bearing witness as to the gruesome finds of human limbs, smoked and hung, with other parts in pickle, ready to provide food for the tribe, and in a ringing voice each of them swore to this swiftly and simply, and to the fact that everything found had now been buried with decency.

So the sentence was passed, the men to be dismembered, even as they had dismembered their victims, and the women and children burned. Here, Lady Margaret felt the sickness to her stomach, yet when her horrified gaze fell on the youngest of the tribe, she could only marvel that they were human and not animal.

" His Majesty could choose a quicker death for the children," she whispered to Archibald. " They have been reared as animals."

" They die as animals," said Sir Archibald. " The youngest of them would destroy thee at a blow, even if reared by the highest in the land. They are savages."

Margaret had a sudden longing for Balgennan, and wondered if they would be allowed to return home next day after the sentences on the wretches were carried out at Leith, but it was not to be. The King felt that they all needed a few days' rest and relaxation after the ordeal of Sawney Bean, and he had commanded that his Court proceed northwards to Greyfriars at Perth.

" Does he play with us, as a cat plays with a mouse?" asked Margaret, and the Earl shook his head.

" Nay, our King is stern, but just. He will throw off his cloak of ruler and play the merry host, rejoicing in games of skill, but he will ever be watchful of us to decide if we are guilty of disloyalty to the Crown, and will keep his own counsel till he has decided. We must pray to God he sees us in true light, and remember to conduct ourselves with decorum."

"I can only be what I am," said Sir Archibald.

"Balgennan is greater than thee," said the Earl, sternly. "Remember that it is through you that we stand in this plight now, even though Sir Gavin did not help."

Lady Margaret said nothing.

Sir Gavin, too, was silent and thinking his own thoughts. He hoped that if the King grew to wrath it would fall on his head alone. But he would defend Lady Helen with his life.

Sir Robert Stewart, whose duty it was to look after the King's household, was gathering his party of men together, prior to riding ahead to Blackfriars, and Sir Gavin watched them riding out of the courtyard and turning north towards the Firth of Forth.

"Tomorrow we all ride north," said the Earl, "but for now we remain in Edinburgh this night."

There was food being provided for the King, Queen Johanna and all the royal household and courtiers, but Margaret felt her appetite had deserted her as, she saw, it had deserted more than one. The day's doings were sour to their stomachs. She was glad to retire with the other women and lose a little of the day's activities in restless sleep.

*   *   *

The King, too, was restless and unusually impatient with his Queen when she demurred about the journey to Blackfriars.

"Have you forgotten that old Highland woman's prophesy?" she asked, "that if you cross water, you will never return. The Firth of Forth is water, and it maun be crossed if we ride to Blackfriars."

"A tale from a demented old woman!" he cried. "I have forgotten her and pay small heed to her prophecies. I will see you grow into old woman yourself, if you believe the tale."

" If I believe the tale, you will not see me age, nor yet thy son who is but six. Let us stay in Linlithgow, Sire, which is ever more beautiful now, with richness of hangings and fine furniture."

" When I asked the King of England, your Cousin Henry, for your hand, I promised a palace worthy of a Beaufort. I always keep my promises."

" But . . . "

" I keep this one, that we ride to Blackfriars with the Court. I maun have decisions to make, and I want to be sure I am right. Decisions are easy against an enemy, but hard when they would shake at the solid grounds of friendship, or what *seems* like friendship. I maun be wise to tell the difference. At Blackfriars I will be able to limber up my body with some good games of tennis, a game I love, and so limber up my mind. Hush thee, my dove. Your own spirits need a fresh breeze blowing them bright again. The rogues and villains we have witnessed have poured out their foulness over you and dulled your well-being."

" Very well, Sire. So be it."

She shrugged with resignation, and called her serving maid to bed her. The King would follow after a short time at his devotions and meditation.

There was no room for two Kings in the land, thought James, and he had disposed of the Albanys, but now they still came to plague and haunt him, even in the guise of a young girl, no doubt beautiful as a dove, but protected by Balgennan's son, and the Squire . . . two fine young men such as he needed in his Kingdom.

James rubbed his hand over his eyes wearily. He sat up reading despatches which had come from England by a secret route. The young King Henry VI was too young to reign and already the Beauforts, relatives of his own Queen, were gaining power. Cardinal Beaufort was very rich, and was powerful opposition to Duke Humphrey of Gloucester, who was Regent for the young Prince.

James' lip curled. He had precious little time for Duke

173

Humphrey. There was still hatred between Scotland and England, but as a boy he had admired the courage and bravery of Henry V, and all he had fought for in France, and had even aided his army with his own. But now it was all like to vanish as snow in sunshine. The Duke of Burgundy was making his peace with France, Bedford was dead, and the English troops were leaving Paris with the mob hooting after them. Was this what happened to victory after the victor departed this life? Would his own victory in pulling his country together and uniting the warring Clans for the good of the whole country be as ephemeral, and would the country once again be split apart, with some of his Nobles grabbing for power, should he die before his son was old enough to reign?

James felt as though he were enveloped in a blanket of shivering fear, then he put it from him, and deliberately stamped around, throwing off his shakes. The day's deeds had been necessary, but the whole business had been unsavoury. He vowed he would not ponder any longer on the problems which teased his mind. He would keep an eye on Balgennan, and watch young Johnson of Nithrie, to see if they deserved punishment . . . along with the girl . . . Albany's girl.

Yet, if there was a child . . . a new generation . . .

King James paused again, and rubbed his forehead. It would still have to be pondered carefully. It was long past time to retire, however, and wearily he put his thoughts to sleep, and crept into the royal bedchamber, where the Queen lay awake, listening intently, then dropped into slumber.

SEVENTEEN

Margaret did not like the Blackfriars Monastery at Perth. It felt cold and bleak in the chill of a February day, the bleakest of all months. The King was a man of many moods, stern ruler, poetic Prince, musician and sportsman. It was this latter which attracted Archibald, and he found he was well matched with His Majesty in a game of tennis.

Margaret had earlier watched with the other ladies while the Nobles played vigorously, their breath moisturising in the cold air.

"They will be laid low with the ague," she said to Lady Catherine Douglas, "having their sweats cooled by the wind. Does it not strike you to the heart, Lady Catherine, as a cold place."

"It is ever warmed by the devotions," laughed Lady Catherine, "and by the laughter of the children. See how the young Prince watches his father's every stroke while the Princesses seem to do nothing else but earn chastisement in their quarrels. I declare Queen Johanna is like to spoil them."

"She has been happy as Queen of Scotland, has she not?" asked Lady Margaret, broodingly.

"Indeed Her Majesty has been happy," Lady Catherine was saying. "She and the King made a love match, and he was granted her hand in marriage, by the consent of King Henry, and her father, the Duke of Somerset. Surely this is not news to thee, Lady Margaret."

She shook her head, her eyes on Sir Archibald. He was almost as big and broad as the King, and although she had felt sickened when she saw the in-breeding of the Sawney Bean gang, the cold bracing air and rich table was beginning to put new life into her, and her eyes were again on her husband. Sir Archibald was going to stand no more vapours, or so he had promised her, and for a while she had felt the glow of well-being in her limbs, though there was still shadows in her heart. She had caught her husband's eyes on her and knew that their passion would be great. Did she want her heart warmed to bursting, then have it cooled in prison during His Majesty's pleasure, for aiding Nell Stewart?

"What ails thee?" asked Lady Catherine. "A fine robust girl. Why are there no heirs to Balgennan?"

"Do you think it matters that Sir Archibald is my true cousin?" she asked.

"What are you asking?"

"I am a-feared that . . . that our children may be imbecile with in-breeding like . . . like the cannibal clan."

"If so, then half of the fine families in Europe are imbeciles, and look to the English Crown for examples among the Royal household. Is thy childless state your own wish, or . . . ?"

"My own wish," said Margaret. "My husband ailed when we first wed, then . . . then I feared our union would not breed well."

Lady Catherine watched the tennis match, her eyes going to two stone masons who were blocking up a hole in the wall to prevent the loss of the King's tennis balls.

"I would have no such fears in your position. He is a fine man, and giving His Majesty a fair game, such as he loves. He demands obedience to authority, but in sportsmanship, he demands fair play."

Sir Robert Stewart crossed the courtyard, and Margaret shivered a little.

"I know not what ails me, but I feel the chill in my heart. The good Sir Robert sees well to His Majesty's household, but his eye upon me makes shivers to my stomach."

"Ah . . . the good Sir Robert Stewart," laughed Lady Catherine, "and ever an eye for a pretty maid. He would be sad to hear thy flattery!"

"The fault is in me," said Margaret, penitently. "Since we fought with those evil creatures and cave dwellers, I have felt no inner peace, yet my heart should settle now that I know the fate of my dear sister, though it grieves me to remember her so. Yet even now I sense the evil still surrounding me . . ."

"Hush thee," warned Lady Catherine, "else we will feel that witchcraft has entered thy soul."

"I am no witch," said Margaret. "My enemy was a witch."

"Tonight there is feasting and merry-making," said Lady Catherine. "Tonight we sit at the King's table and wear a gown of velvet and pearls with fine embroidery, to make the King and Queen feel happy. He is ever a believer that the quickest way to a dull mind is to keep the spirit dull. See to it that your young Lord is swift to enjoy the King's sallies, and all will be well."

*　　　*　　　*

Sir Gavin sought out Margaret as the courtiers were all preparing to assemble for evening prayers. The Queen had asked for the ladies to have short prayers earlier in the day in the Lady's Chapel, the cold being enough to soak through their silks and velvets, to the marrow of their bones.

"Lady Margaret," Gavin whispered, urgently. "Have ye time for a quiet word? It is urgent."

"What ails thee, Sir Gavin," she asked, seeing the white face and staring eyes of the young Baron.

"I know not for sure, but there is something stirring, and I am a-feared it may be a trap for the Earl, and those of us who owe allegiance to his House. I have watched the eyes of the serving men who have been about their duties, and they go examining the door locks, not to mention a party I saw kneeling down near to the drawbridge. I think it is intended to seize us, and imprison us, while we are at the mercy of His Majesty, and before we can find friends to help us."

Margaret felt her heart bound in fear. She had been aware of a coldness and hostility about Blackfriars from the moment she set foot in the place.

177

"Your nerves are shaken, Sir Gavin," she said. "The King has ever been pleasant to the Earl, and treats him with kindness. Is it not your own imaginings?"

Gavin shook his head.

"I like not the looks of the Steward, Sir Robert Stewart, who is ever watchful of my doings, and who has decreed that we all attend Vespers. It would be easy to seize the Earl, Sir Archibald and myself while the Courtiers are at their devotions, and the ladies in merry mood together, then those who would befriend us will find it is too late to plead for us. We will be beyond anyone's help, unless I do something now. My Lady, I plan to slip away and ride for Nithrie. I can claim that I ride fast as a King's messenger on behalf of a requisite for the Royal children, and my face is well known to the Guard, and maybe I will be believed, if I show the urgency I feel.

"But if the Guards have already been told, I am lost, as are we all, and it will make no difference, since we are lost anyway."

Suddenly Lady Margaret felt her inner being growing painful with anguish, and she longed for her husband, Sir Archibald. She thought of the many times she had repulsed him, and now she would fain have his arms holding her in love. In this hour when she, too, felt the smell of danger all round them, she knew that her passion was all for her husband, and wept inwardly for all the days and nights they could have shared in close comfort together. Now her life might be torn from her before she had lived it to the full.

"What are your plans?" she asked Sir Gavin.

"To ride for Nithrie and take the Lady Helen over the Border, and if I could have a note of fealty from thee to thy household in Cumberland, we may yet be safe. With Lady Helen well out of harm's way, the King could not accuse Balgennan of harbouring her. Nor could he harm her, as he would do, if he knew she is with child."

"If we cause the King's displeasure, it may be the greater when he finds she is no longer at Nithrie."

"He can declare us banished, and put us to the horn, and we

dared not return to Scotland. My young brother, who is but six years old, can become Master of Nithrie, and I give up my Barony. I will offer my fealty to Henry, and serve as a soldier to earn a patch of land for my wife and my children."

" It is well enough reasoned," said Lady Margaret. " If your feelings are true ones . . . and I do not deny those fears since they are my own. Go quickly, and I will find Sir Archibald. Have you told him of your plans?"

Sir Gavin shook his head.

" He would try to fight it out bravely, and be killed for his courage. I go by stealth, and dare not risk an open challenge."

" My prayers go with you," said Margaret, as she slipped a ring into his hand. " There is no time for a letter, but this was my mother's ring. She will welcome you if it is presented to her kindly. Do not wound her by telling her of the Galloway mob. I would keep her in ignorance of that horror. God guard thee."

" God guard thee," whispered Sir Gavin, and slid away into the shadows.

*   *   *

Margaret hurried to their quarters, where Archibald had cleansed himself after his strenuous games with the King, and robed well in wool under his rich velvet tunic, against the cold of the chapel. Margaret thought him the most magnificent man she had ever seen, and wondered that his strong dominant face had ever repelled her, or that she could have seen ugliness where now there was only beauty.

" I go to Vespers," he told her, picking up his cloak.

" I know, my heart," she replied, and he turned to stare at her, seeing the softness of love in her eyes.

" What is this?" he asked. " A change of heart? You are a wayward woman, I vow. You were warm to me, then cold when I would have taken you. Now there is warmth when the Chapel bells call us to prayers."

" There is no time," she said, urgently, " but I sense danger for us. I just wanted to tell you that . . . that should we be parted, it will be as though my body were rent apart, and that my love is all for you. I beg forgiveness for having denied you, and I deserved to have been beaten, and forced. Now . . . now I have fears in my heart, and it may be too late . . ."

Sir Archibald laughed joyously and caught her in his arms, kissing her with gentleness, then with great passion, holding her close as though to give warmth and protection.

" It is the cold, my heart, but rest assured that the cold is over for us. I will warm you with my love and there will be no room for complaint, that I promise you. Beg leave to retire early, my dove. We make up for lost time."

Margaret felt a surge of happiness and blind hope that Gavin had been wrong. If the King was not displeased with them, and they returned to Balgennan in two days time, then her heart would indeed take wing. She thought of the old Castle with the rich sound of the ocean breaking against the rocks under the Castle walls, and the seagulls crying plaintively as the sunshine caught a curve of their white wings.

The Earl was already calling to Archibald that the bell had sounded, and with a quick hug, he left her to walk down the long cold corridor.

Margaret made her way slowly to the Great Hall where a fire burned brightly, though it was not enough to warm the air throughout.

The King was with the ladies, having excused himself from devotions since his games had tired him, at the instigation of Sir Robert Stewart who encouraged him to relax and be entertained by the ladies, and to entertain them by reading his latest poems.

Margaret saw his eyes rest on her, but they showed no hostility, and her spirits lifted. Sir Gavin was wrong to sense danger. It was his own nervous fear and imaginings and he, in turn, had passed on that fear to her. His wife's pregnancy was making an old woman out of him, she thought, amused.

" Come, make way for my Lady Johnson," the King said, and the ladies formed a group round His Majesty who wore a garnet velvet tunic, laced at the neck, over a shirt of finest wool. Many of the ladies were wearing elaborately designed gowns which were being much admired.

" We make fine clothes when our lords do not go to war," Lady Catherine Douglas was saying, " otherwise we maun spend our time repairing torn raiment and some of us would defend our Keeps with our lives."

" As it should be," said the King. " A woman is no less brave for being a woman, and would defend her young more fiercely than a man. Is it not so, my own?" he asked, turned to the Queen.

" It is so."

Margaret's new happiness in the love she bore for her husband and his for her, had made her more aware of love in others, and she marvelled at the bond between the King and his Queen. Surely this fine cultured man could not be hatching treachery against his well-tried servants and friends.

He was in high good humour, much recovered from his fatigue after a day of exercise. Sir Robert Stewart's notion that he should relax with the Queen and her ladies had been a good one. He liked the sparkling brightness of their company, and was only too happy to play to the ladies, and read them a few more verses from " A King's Quair."

Along the corridor from the Great Hall, Margaret could hear the servants busy about their duties, and the voice of Sir Robert as he shouted orders for them to obey. Why did her flesh creep when she was close to the man, she wondered? He was ever quiet, and cat-like in his movements.

Suddenly her eyes were on the bar which would lock the door against intruders, though this night no one was an intruder. Soon the men would join the ladies, leaving solemn affairs of Church and State aside, and there would be dancing and merry-making enough to warm them and make them forget the cold of a winter's night.

Margaret found her eyes straying to the door, wishing the time to pass quickly, when Sir Archibald would be back from his devotions, and would come to stand by her side, the warmth of his body next to her own, his fingers reaching out to take her hand.

Yet there was something wrong with the door. The bar should have shown up as a black mass against the solid door, even in the glowing light of the candles. But it was not there!

Margaret considered it curiously while the King's voice lulled them with the beauty and imagery of his poetry. It was little wonder that Queen Johanna loved him, she thought, when he could find the softness of such words in his soul. If her own inner excitement had not been so great, she might have been lost in the poem instead of studying the door.

Yet even as she watched, she could hear the raised voices of a disturbance further along the corridor and the raucous voice of a man, shouting out commands.

" That's Graham," cried the King, starting up, " the Tutor of Strathearn . . . what does he mean by coming here this e'en? Who allowed him to cross the drawbridge when I gave orders that I did not wish to be disturbed, except for messages of great urgency. Graham is no such messenger."

Margaret and Lady Catherine Douglas had walked across to the door.

" Look!" said Margaret. " The lock is spoiled. The bar across has been broken."

Even as she said the words, they could hear the clash of armoured men in the corridor, and Margaret fell back, her heart failing her. So it was true! Tonight she would lay down her head in a prison cell. There would be no passionate love with her husband. There would be swords and armoury between them, not love.

Then Lady Catherine had bounded forward, putting her arm through the lock, even as the soldiers were at the door.

" What ails thee?" she called, loudly.

" We come to demand the person of the King," called Sir Robert Graham, " who is no King to his people, but tyrant and murderer."

" He is not here!" Catherine called. " This is a company of the Queen and her ladies. Thee are no Knight, Sir, if thee would break into her privacy."

In a low voice she commanded Margaret:

'Quick, my Lady. The King is unarmed. Under that floor rug there is a trapdoor . . . help His Majesty."

The King had seized a pair of heavy tongs which had just been used on the fire, and in a trice he had levered up the plank of wood under the floor rug, and dropped into the vault under the room, while Margaret and one of the other ladies replaced the rug on top of the closed wooden plank.

"Thank God," whispered the Queen, her face paper-white, her whole body shaking with terror. "He can escape through a hole in the outer wall."

"He cannot, Majesty," the other lady said, white to the lips. "The King had the hole blocked only this day, since his tennis balls were lost there."

"Then we maun pray that they do not find him," said the Queen, "because if they do . . . "

Her eyes glittered strangely, and a moment later they all cried out with terror as the door was flung open and Lady Catherine Douglas staggered back, her arm broken, the pain searing her so that she fell, senseless, to the floor.

"What is the meaning of this outrage?" cried the Queen. "The King is not here!"

"Hold thy tongue, woman," said Sir Robert Graham, his eyes staring as one demented. "We know he is here. The good Sir Robert Stewart, my true friend, has made sure he is here, and now we maun find the petticoat which hides him."

"Traitor!" screamed the Queen, and he struck her fiercely across the cheek while his soldiers treated the women roughly, handling them with malicious glee saying they maun be sure there was no gentlemanly body beneath their skirts and finery.

Margaret fought off a young ruffian whose hand had grabbed at her breast, and was ready to lift a hot coal from the fire to thrust in his face, when Graham called them to order, searching the wall hangings and pulling over cabinets even though it was clear to see they hid nought.

The ladies held their breath, too frozen with fear even to cry out, and Margaret prayed that Vespers would soon be over, and the Courtiers hear the disturbance, though the

Chapel of the Monastery was well away from the living quarters.

It had been well timed, she thought bitterly, remembering how Sir Gavin had sensed something was wrong seeing men examining the locks and the drawbridge. Then there was her own distrust of Sir Robert Stewart, which had been well founded. He had spoiled the locks, removed the Courtiers and, as she discovered later, laid planks over the drawbridge to admit Sir Robert Graham and his men. The plot had been well laid, but looked as though it was going to meet with failure.

Knowing now that the King had meant no harm to Balgennan, sudden fierce loyalty filled her heart, and she held her breath, praying for the King's deliverance. He was a true leader for their country, and already Scotland was forgeing ahead, and becoming a new and graciously beautiful land under his guidance. His strength kept the peace, and his delicacy brought grace and dignity to the lives of his people.

She was standing on the rug which covered the plank, then suddenly she was thrust aside, and with a horrified cry, she saw the soldiers testing the planks with their swords.

The Queen swooned in a dead faint as one of the murderers prised up the plank, then leapt down into the vault, and they could hear the King shout, then the cry of the man as the King had him by the throat, throwing him to the ground.

Then Sir Robert Graham strode forward, and leapt into the vault, his sword drawn against an unarmed man, and his King.

" I beg thee to let us fight like men," cried the King, weary with his struggles against the first soldier. " Give me a sword and we will fight fair."

" Fight fair! " cried Sir Robert. " Who are *thee* to talk of fair fighting, thee who has had no mercy on others, and will get none from me."

Margaret could see Graham thrusting his sword into the King's body, then two other of his men leapt down and each of them stabbed repeatedly at the dying King.

Margaret ran to the door, hearing the sounds of the Courtiers returning, then as Sir Archibald realised what was happening, he was marshalling his men and alerting the other Nobles.

But it was too late for King James I, and his grief-stricken Queen Johanna.

" I will never rest," the Queen vowed, " until I have had my revenge, and the King's. I will never rest until they have been punished tenfold."

EIGHTEEN

It seemed to Lady Margaret, as she rode back to Balgennan a few days later beside the Earl and Sir Archibald, that she had lived a lifetime in those few short days. They had been days of terrible retribution inflicted on Sir Robert Graham, as the Queen had grown into a tigress in her rage, grief and hate.

Margaret shuddered when she thought of the tortures inflicted on the men responsible for the King's death, and knew that even the most hardened Nobles, used to inflicting punishment on wrong-doers, had had little stomach for the torture Sir Robert Graham had to endure, and for the bravery and defiance he showed to the last, believing that what he had done was right.

"Female animals have more cruelty lying within their hearts," Archibald had said. "Truly their wrath is terrible, no doubt born in them to help with the defence of their young."

Margaret had been too depressed to agree or disagree. The body of Sir Gavin Johnson had been found near the draw-bridge, either killed by Graham's men as they stealthily walked across the boards put down by Sir Robert Stewart, to prevent raising the alarm, or murdered by the Queen's men believing him to be part of the plot. The Early wept silently when he saw the dead boy whom he had grown to love like a son, as had Margaret, remembering as she did her first few months at Balgennan, and how much she had held the Squire in love and respect.

"At least his wife will be safe now at Nithrie," said Margaret to Archibald, "and there will be an heir to the Barony. Sir

Gavin, brave Knight, would have laid down his life to defend her. Now that the King is dead, there is no one to demand more retribution of the Albanys. The Queen has her own hates to attend to with the Grahams and Sir Robert Stewart. No wonder I felt cold in his presence. He was indeed a traitor."

"I will ride to Nithrie as soon as we return to Balgennan," said Sir Archibald. "It is sad news for my kinsman and his family, but they will be proud that Sir Gavin died bravely, giving his life for his family when I tell them so."

"For that I honour you the more, my heart," said Margaret.

*　　*　　*

The Queen had sought the support of Sir William Crichton, remembering the advice her dead husband and King had given her, and wishing him to take guardianship of her little son, James, who had just celebrated his sixth birthday. She knew she would be unable to reign as Regent, and keep the country together in the same way that James had done. And in any case, the light had gone out of her life with his death.

Margaret would never forget the anguish of the widowed Queen, but felt that her sorrow and hate had deprived her of reason.

"I fear that we maun strengthen our defences at Balgennan," the Earl said, as they rode home again. "I feel the unrest blowing up, and we maun be on the lookout for the Douglases who would seize power till wee James is of an age. There is too much jealousy among the Earls and Barons. They are forever keeking at one another's property and remembering slights done by their ancestors, one to another. The King's death is a sad blow to this country, and a fearsome setback."

Riding beside him, Sir Archibald nodded, agreeing with his father that there would be troubled times ahead.

"When did we not have troubled times?" he countered. "For Balgennan they might have been even more troubled. Have you forgotten that we could have been cooling our heels, well chastised, in one of His Majesty's prisons, while he destroyed our kinsmen at Nithrie, if the fancy had taken him?"

"No, he had reasoned things to our good," said Margaret. "I'm sure of that."

"He could have had second thoughts, after the heir to Nithrie was born," said Archibald. "It would have hung over our heads like a sword."

Suddenly they were within sight of their own fair Castle, with the seagulls screaming their joy, their wings glinting like frosted snow in the winter sunshine. The pure air filled Archibald's lungs as he turned to his lady, seeing that she was beautiful beyond any woman he had ever seen, and that she was as brave and proud a lady as any he could have wished for Balgennan.

Together they would have an heir who would guard their heritage, and their Kingdom against troubled times, even as they rejoiced in settled peace. On the peaceful hill pastures, sheep grazed from a labourer's cottage, a wisp of smoke rose into the air. It was a land which had caught Margaret's heart, and held it.

"Come, my dove," said Archibald. "We ride home together."

The Earl smiled as he watched them gallop ahead of him, then he signed to his men and he, too, spurred his horse.

He was well pleased with his heir.